"I need you for protection."

He waited for her to start making sense. "Go on."

She moistened her lips. This sounded so damn melodramatic, she thought, but it was all true. "I need you to help me steal my son back."

"Then you do know who has him." He'd had a feeling all along that she did.

She nodded. "I think so."

"Look, Ms. Armstrong, if this is some kind of a custody battle, you need a lawyer, not me."

"No," Dakota insisted, "I need you. Or more accurately put, what I need is a hero." She turned on all of her considerable charm. "Will you be my hero, Andreini?"

Dear Reader,

Once again, Silhouette Intimate Moments brings you six exciting romances, a perfect excuse to take a break and read to your heart's content. Start off with *Heart of a Hero*, the latest in award-winning Marie Ferrarella's CHILDFINDERS, INC. miniseries. You'll be on the edge of your seat as you root for the heroine to find her missing son—and discover true love along the way. Then check out the newest of our FIRSTBORN SONS, *Born Brave*, by Ruth Wind, another of the award winners who make Intimate Moments so great every month. In Officer Hawk Stone you'll discover a hero any woman—and that includes our heroine!—would fall in love with.

Cassidy and the Princess, the latest from Patricia Potter, is a gripping story of a true princess of the ice and the hero who lures her in from the cold. With *Hard To Handle*, mistress of sensuality Kylie Brant begins CHARMED AND DANGEROUS, a trilogy about three irresistible heroes and the heroines lucky enough to land them. Be sure to look for her again next month, when she takes a different tack and contributes our FIRSTBORN SONS title. Round out the month with new titles from up-and-comers Shelley Cooper, whose *Promises, Promises* offers a new twist on the pregnant-heroine plot, and Wendy Rosnau, who tells a terrific amnesia story in *The Right Side of the Law*.

And, of course, come back again next month, when the romantic roller-coaster ride continues with six more of the most exciting romances around.

Enjoy!

Leslie J. Wainger
Executive Senior Editor

Please address questions and book requests to:
Silhouette Reader Service
U.S.: 3010 Walden Ave., P.O. Box 1325, Buffalo, NY 14269
Canadian: P.O. Box 609, Fort Erie, Ont. L2A 5X3

Heart of
a Hero

MARIE
FERRARELLA

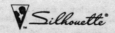

INTIMATE MOMENTS™

Published by Silhouette Books

America's Publisher of Contemporary Romance

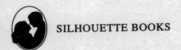 SILHOUETTE BOOKS

ISBN 0-373-27175-1

HEART OF A HERO

Copyright © 2001 by Marie Rydzynski-Ferrarella

This edition published by arrangement with Harlequin Books S.A.

Visit Silhouette at www.eHarlequin.com

Printed in U.S.A.

Books by Marie Ferrarella in Miniseries

MARIE FERRARELLA

earned a master's degree in Shakespearean comedy and, perhaps as a result, her writing is distinguished by humor and natural dialogue. This RITA Award-winning author has one goal: to entertain, to make people laugh and feel good. She has written over a hundred books for Silhouette, some under the name Marie Nicole. Her romances are beloved by fans worldwide and have been translated into Spanish, Italian, German, Russian, Polish, Japanese and Korean.

1/1/2001
To my family,
May this be the beginning
of
something wonderful.

Chapter 1

The scream filled the area around him.

Eyes he hadn't realized he'd shut flew open as the sound registered in his brain. Restoring the recliner he'd just dropped into less than ten minutes ago to its original upright position, Russell Andreini cocked his head and listened intently to make sure he hadn't just dreamed the jarring sound. But even as he strained to hear, Rusty was getting to his feet.

The scream, he was almost certain, had come from the garden apartment just below his own. It hadn't originated from a television set in the vicinity turned up too loud, or from some ridiculous radio commercial meant to catch your attention. It had come from a woman.

A very terrified woman.

Rusty was beyond bone-weary. He had come home

after putting in eighteen hours of surveillance that had led to a gratifying payoff just two hours ago and was more than entitled to feel the way he did. But, like the professional he was, Rusty forgot his exhaustion as adrenaline began to surge through his body.

He was willing to bet a month of his sister Megan's Sunday steaks that the scream had come from the blonde directly below him.

Not stopping for the shoes he'd carelessly discarded when he'd walked into his apartment, Rusty yanked open his front door.

The echoes of the first scream were just fading from his head when he heard a second one.

Hands braced on the balustrades on either side of him, he sailed down the narrow stone steps that led to the ground level.

He was right, the scream had come from the apartment directly below his. Most likely from the woman who'd never returned his smile the few times their paths had crossed. He had to pass her door each time he either came down or went up the stairs that led to his own apartment.

As near as he remembered, the woman had moved in about a month ago and spoke to no one. He'd once seen her in the laundry room and tried to start up a conversation. After a lengthy pause she'd responded with a monosyllabic sentence, dumped her soiled laundry back into her basket and, taking the hand of the little boy who seemed never to be far out of her reach, made a hasty exit.

Rusty recalled glancing at his watch, noting that

the woman had hurried away less than three minutes after he'd entered the laundry room. She'd made him wonder.

She seemed far too young and attractive to appear so solemn-eyed and distant. And though the green eyes she'd turned up to him had been hard, he thought he'd detected fear beneath the wariness. That had made him wonder, too. He never liked seeing anyone in pain.

"Hey, everything all right in there?" Rusty called as he knocked loudly on the woman's door. The only response was another scream. "Dumb question," Rusty mumbled under his breath as he tried the doorknob.

The door was locked. He glanced around to see if anyone else had heard the screams and was coming to help, but apparently everyone else in the complex had a life they were attending to. There were very few lights on within the surrounding apartments. It was Friday night and the residents in the complex were predominantly single. In all likelihood, they were all out enjoying themselves.

"Open up. It's Rusty." He added as a clarifying afterthought, "From upstairs."

He'd introduced himself to her during their run-in in the laundry room. Etiquette notwithstanding, she hadn't felt the need to tell him her name in return. When he'd tried to talk to her son, a boy he judged to be around two, she'd scooped the boy up and quickly retreated from the area. The brunette who'd been quick to take up her space had also tried to fill her place in the conversation, being far more communicative than her predecessor.

Rusty had fallen into the conversation easily, even though he'd been distracted by the woman who'd walked out so quickly with her son. People usually found him incredibly easy to talk to and he had wonderful rapport with kids. The whole incident had taken him somewhat aback.

But he figured his silent neighbor had her reasons and he wasn't the kind to pry, at least, not in his private life. He did enough of that professionally.

When there was no response to his pounding, Rusty called out again. "Ma'am?"

This time there was no scream, no answer. At least, no answer that fell under the heading of human. It was just a keening sound that sliced through him, going clear down to the bone. Cutting into him far more than even the scream had.

He'd only heard such pain once before. When his mother had realized that someone had kidnapped Chad.

Without pausing to think, Rusty backed up, then rammed his shoulder into the door as hard as he could. The door groaned and then finally gave, slamming against the opposite wall.

In a delayed reaction, pain shot through his shoulder like an exploding grenade.

Somewhere in the back of his mind it occurred to Rusty that breaking down a door, or at least forcing it open always looked a great deal easier when the hero did it in the movies or on TV.

Real life was a whole lot harder. But then, he already knew that.

Rusty scanned the area. The apartment layout was a carbon copy of his own. There was a tiny kitchen with a square table immediately to his left and a small living room directly in front of him. Neither was occupied. He raced to the back of the apartment. There was a room on either end of the abbreviated hall.

He found her in the smaller of the two.

Rusty saw why the screams had momentarily halted. Barefoot, wearing a thigh-length, cotton-candy-pink nightgown, the woman was covering her mouth with both hands. Her eyes were opened so wide with shock and terror that for a second he said nothing, afraid of setting her off.

The empty wooden crib in the corner registered belatedly.

The next moment, as if suddenly becoming aware of the fact that she was no longer alone, the woman grabbed up the small, free-standing lamp and grasped it in both hands, prepared to wield it like some sort of martial arts weapon.

''What did you do with him?'' she demanded. The terror he'd seen in her eyes a heartbeat ago was replaced with anger. ''Damn it, answer me! Where is he? Where's Vinny?''

Rusty stood a healthy distance from the woman, wondering how best to disarm her without risking hurting her. He'd seen that look before, more times in the last couple of years than he would have liked to think about. It was the look of a mother forcibly separated from her child.

"Your son?" he asked needlessly, his voice low, soothing. It was the kind of tone used by an animal tamer trying to gentle a crazed animal that had been abused.

Except it wasn't working. If anything, she looked even more incensed. She took a step back, her eyes never leaving his.

"You know damn well who I'm talking about," she snapped, her hands tightening around the shank of the lamp, her manner growing more desperate. "Yes, my son. Now what have you done with him?" She'd just barely managed to keep from screaming into his face.

Who the hell was this man and what was he doing here? How had he managed to "conveniently" come along just at this moment?

Was he part of it?

Her heart pounding madly, afraid to turn her back on him, she eyed him the way someone would a pit bull that had suddenly appeared in their path.

Spreading his hands wide on either side of his six-foot-three lanky body, Rusty took only a half step forward. He kept his eye on the lamp, afraid she might wind up hurting herself more than him.

"I haven't done anything with him. Lady, I was just nodding off when I heard you scream." His expression still open, affable, his tone sharpened just a shade, instantly becoming authoritative. "What happened?"

She looked as if she wasn't sure if he was telling the truth, or if she should trust him. It was apparent to Rusty that if she was going to let her guard down, it wouldn't be too far.

Her eyes wary as she watched him, she finally inclined her head toward the empty crib. "I came in to check on Vinny before I went to bed and...and..."

"He wasn't there?" Rusty supplied gently, moved by the anguish he heard beneath the bravado. Empathy had always been his gift. It had sharpened considerably since he'd found his vocation in life.

Exercising supreme effort, Dakota Armstrong struggled to pull herself together. She wasn't going to do her son any good if she fell apart the way she so dearly wanted to. But, God, she was tired, so tired. Tired of running and hiding. Tired of always looking over her shoulder, of being suspicious and weighing every word, every look, that came her way.

She couldn't fall apart, she told herself again. She was all Vinny had and he needed her. Now more than ever. Needed her to save him before he was forever lost. Lost to her and to himself.

Tossing the sea of blond hair over her shoulder with a quick movement of her head, she echoed Rusty's words. "He wasn't there."

There were questions, a whole host of questions that sprang up instantly, crowding his brain. But rather than ask them, Rusty hurried past the woman to look out the open window. At first glance, there was nothing.

Bracing his hand on the windowsill, he lowered

himself out. The questions would keep until later. Right now, every second that went by might be precious. It was the first thing he'd been taught.

Wood creaked beneath his foot. Outside each ground-floor apartment that faced the inside of the complex there was a small wooden structure that served as a pseudo-bridge. The bridge, which stretched picturesquely over a minuscule pond, took the place of the patio awarded to the second-floor occupants.

Rusty held his breath as he looked around. Visibility was limited. There were no stars out, no moonlight. Illumination came from the tall street lamps scattered equidistantly throughout the 110-unit complex. He saw no one out walking, much less running from the apartment or in the general vicinity.

Except for the artificially induced gurgling of the water within each pond, the entire area was quieter than a tomb.

Turning back toward the window, he felt his sock catch on a sliver of wood. He stooped to work it free and glanced down. Right next to the wooden bridge, just beyond the window, was a footprint in the mud. A sneaker, as best he could tell. Squinting, he tried to examine the print and decided that he would need a flashlight.

Without a flashlight, all he could tell was that the print was elongated, as if someone had slipped before regaining his or her footing. And it appeared to be fresh.

Rusty lowered himself back into the missing boy's

bedroom. He would have expected to find the woman on the telephone, calling the police. Instead she was standing in the center of the room, just as he had left her, looking not unlike a lost waif herself. She had her arms wrapped around herself, as if she was mutely trying to offer herself comfort.

Backlit by the lamp she'd returned to its original position on the floor, the nightgown she was wearing was translucent. Every inch of her long, supple body was highlighted.

Rusty felt his mouth suddenly grow drier than dust. It took him a beat before he found his thoughts and put them into some kind of coherent order. "There's no one out there."

She moved past him to the window and looked out. The same window she'd looked out before without any success. This man in her apartment wasn't saying anything to her she didn't already know.

Still, she clung to denial.

"There has to be," she cried. "Vinny couldn't have climbed through the window himself." She swung around from the window to glare accusingly. "They took him."

She said it as if she had someone in mind, Rusty thought. Did she? "'They'?"

Maybe it was his imagination, but her shoulders seemed to stiffen at his question.

"The kidnappers," she amended. "Whoever took my baby."

Maybe now was the time to start questioning her in earnest. "When did you last see your son?"

He saw her struggle to try to think, to push aside the confusion and shock that he knew had taken hold of her. She put her hand to her head as if that could help sort out the answer.

"An hour and a half ago."

There were tears shining in her eyes. And then they began to wet her lashes, about to spill out.

Angry with herself, she wiped them away with the heel of her hand. More came.

What Rusty did next was second nature to him. He took her into his arms and gently held her against him, comforting her. She was someone in need, suffering from shock, and he wanted to help.

For a moment she seemed to soften against him, all but dissolving as she accepted the silent offering. The next moment she jerked back as if she'd suddenly realized what she was doing. Her back stiffened like soldiers' facing down the enemy.

Taken by surprise at the sudden change, Rusty managed to act as if her behavior were perfectly normal. In some ways, he supposed that it was. Disorientation and denial took on many forms. This kind of thing never failed to leave a parent in emotional shambles, strong one minute, crumbling the next. Needing sedation was a common enough occurrence, but he had a feeling that the woman in front of him would not be one of those who found solace that way.

He looked around. "Where's your phone?"

"In the kitchen." Her response was automatic. "Why?"

That should have been evident to her, but then that

wasn't factoring in disorientation. ''You need to call the police.''

Dakota's mouth dropped open. Calling the police was the last thing she wanted to do. There was no doubt in her mind that if she so much as dialed 9-1-1, she'd never see Vinny again.

She rushed after him, trying to get in front of him, to reach the telephone on the wall before he did.

She just made it. ''No!''

Dakota quickly covered the receiver with her hand in case the word hadn't sunk in.

Rusty looked at the fingers splayed over the receiver. As if her small hand could possibly pose a physical deterrent. A tinge of amusement wafted through him. He banked it down.

What was traveling through him in far larger waves was curiosity. Why was she so adamant about not calling in the police? Was she a fugitive of some sort? On the run from someone?

Maybe she was someone's estranged wife who'd suddenly taken off with her child, snatching him away from her husband. Either explanation would go a long way toward accounting for the wariness he'd perceived each time their paths had crossed.

He let his hand drop from the air as he studied her. ''Why don't you want to call the police?''

Her eyes narrowed. She saw no reason to have to explain herself to this man. Not that she would have, anyway. Trusting people was a waste of time and she'd learned a long time ago that depending on anyone just left her open to betrayal and despair.

"Because I just don't, all right?" Suddenly aware that she was standing there in nothing but her nightgown, she grabbed a sweater that was draped over the back of a kitchen chair and dragged it on. "What are you, my mother?" She punched her arms through the sleeves. "Who are you, anyway?"

Rusty shrugged off the hostility directed at him as part of her emotional roller coaster ride she was obviously on.

"I'm the guy who lives upstairs." He jerked a thumb up toward the ceiling, his manner matter-of-fact. "The one you woke up with your screaming."

She appeared to be more in control of herself now than she had even a minute ago. And with that control Rusty saw the hard shell slip back into place, the one he encountered each time he saw her.

"Sorry." She shrugged carelessly. "You can get back to your beauty sleep."

He had no intention of leaving her. Whether or not she admitted it, the woman needed someone to stay with her until a search for her missing son could get properly under way. In his experience, bluster and bravado were common smokescreens for fear.

"Look," he began gently, placing a hand on her shoulder. She shrugged it off as if his touch had burned her very skin. "What are you afraid of?"

"My baby's just been kidnapped, what do you think I'm afraid of?"

He looked at her for a long moment and watched as her body language grew more defensive. Though it wasn't completely uncommon to have someone slip into a house and steal a child from their bed, the method spoke of some degree of familiarity with the victimized family. Which brought him back to the feeling that the kidnapping was the work of someone who knew her, someone who specifically wanted her son. He'd seen the boy and although Vinny was cute, the child was no more or less eye-catching than most other children his age.

No, there had to be more at work here than she was admitting.

He nodded at the telephone, giving every indication of remaining just where he was for the time being. "If you don't want to call the police, maybe you should call your husband."

What did it take to get rid of this man? She needed to be alone. She had to think. She felt as if everything was closing in on her. First Vincent, now Vinny. She'd die before she'd let anyone keep her from her son. And now she had some misguided Good Samaritan—or worse—to deal with. "I don't have a husband."

Rusty glanced at her hand and saw that it was bare of jewelry. There wasn't even a tan line where a wedding ring might once have been.

"Ex-husband, then."

What did it take to get this man to leave her alone? "I don't have one of those, either."

She hadn't conceived her son on her own. "Boyfriend?" He was hazarding guesses now.

Her brows drew together. Of all the cheap tricks. Was this his way of finding out whether there was anyone else living with her? Her son had just been kidnapped, didn't this man have any shame?

"Are you trying to hit on me?" Dakota demanded angrily.

Rusty was calm in the face of her fury. It was in his nature to remain that way. He'd found out a long time ago that losing your head when those around you were losing theirs never accomplished anything.

"No," he told her genially, "just trying to rule out parental kidnapping." To his surprise, he saw her pale slightly.

And then she regrouped as she lifted her chin in a gesture that would have been called defiant by the mildest of observers. Striding over to the door, she threw it open.

"Why don't you just rule yourself out the door if you want to rule out anything?"

The angrier she became, the calmer he remained. "Look, you need help."

She started pacing. He was making her crazy. For all she knew, he was in on it. Just because he had this lean, trustworthy face and soulful blue eyes was no reason to believe a thing he was saying or to buy into his good-neighbor act. She'd been conned by the best.

"No kidding, Sherlock."

Feeling at a loss, fervently wishing that this was all a bad dream, she nervously dragged her hand through her hair.

She'd been so careful to hide her tracks. How had this happened? How had they been found?

When she turned around, she saw the open door

and noted the fact that the man hadn't yet taken the blatant hint and left.

"You want to help? Okay, help." She was new in town, without a single friend to turn to. Not that she would have expected any friend to stand by her. Not when faced with the consequences that friendship entailed. "Tell me where I can find myself a good private detective."

This wasn't making any sense. Most people in her position would have immediately wanted the police to take up the search. Why was she so adamant about not calling them in?

Maybe it was shock, he thought. People in shock did strange things. His sister had handled a case six months ago where the mother insisted on talking to the kidnapped child as if he was right there beside her. There was no question in his mind that if the case hadn't been resolved positively, the woman might have wound up spending the next few years of her life in an institution.

He tried again. "The police—"

How many ways did she have to spell it out? "I said I don't want the police."

"It's a kidnapping," he told her gently, "the police and the FBI have the manpower to blanket the area."

Oh, God, calling in the FBI would be even worse. Vinny would disappear forever. She couldn't do any of that. And this guy, whoever he thought he was, certainly couldn't be allowed to do that, Dakota thought frantically.

"Stop talking to me as if I were an idiot. I know

exactly what'll happen if I call in the police, you don't. No police. No FBI. Nobody on public payroll," she insisted adamantly. "I need someone I can buy, someone who'll work just for me. If you don't know anyone like that—"

Dakota moved to the open front door again, her meaning clear.

He hadn't said anything to her earlier because it would have sounded too opportunistic, as if he were trying to take advantage of the situation and her pain. But since she was insisting on this path, so be it.

Rusty placed his hand on the side of the door and to her annoyed surprise, pushed it closed. "I think it's time I explained to you what I do for a living."

Chapter 2

Her heart stopped beating in her chest.

She stared at the man who had pushed his way into her apartment, into her dilemma. Any second now Dakota was sure her head would spin off if she relinquished the slightest iota of control she was exercising over it. Even now, the room felt as if it had tilted beneath her feet.

What he did for a living?

Dakota's mouth was desert-dry as she whispered, "You're not a cop, are you?"

Until this moment the thought hadn't occurred to her. It should have. The times Andreini had tried to start up a conversation, he'd struck her as being too exuberant, too innocent-looking to be a policeman. But why not? Nothing came in stereotype these days. She of all people should know that by now.

Look at Vincent. She would never have taken him to be who he ultimately turned out to be. Not with that blond hair and that Nordic complexion.

For that matter, look at her. She wasn't what she tried to pretend to be, either. But that was different. That was for survival purposes.

Rusty looked at her more closely. Was it his imagination, or did she look afraid there for a second?

"Not exactly—"

"Then what, exactly?" she cut in before he had a chance to explain anything further.

"I'm a private investigator—"

Her eyes narrowed as she looked at him with contempt. A private investigator. She'd just said she needed one. How convenient.

"Yeah, right."

He couldn't decide whether her contempt was aimed at him or his profession.

"No, I am." To prove it, Rusty dug into his back pocket for his wallet.

Did he have some kind of fake I.D. on him? Something he used to pick up women who thought that kind of a career was cool? Dakota laughed shortly, wondering just how far this man would go with this charade and what kind of a ghoul hit on a woman whose baby had just been stolen.

Her contempt was barely contained. "Pretty big coincidence, don't you think?"

Undeterred, Rusty pulled out his wallet. "Maybe you can think of it as luck."

Enough was enough. She wanted him out of here

so she could think. The fear that she was never going
to see her son again kept washing over her.

"And maybe I can think of it as a scam." Her eyes
narrowed to condemning slits. "Like someone trying
to take advantage of a rotten situation."

He'd been taken with her the second he'd first seen
her walking across the parking lot, her fingers firmly
wrapped around her son's hand. The sway of her hips,
the long, slender legs that seemed to go on forever,
urging a man to follow, and the long mane of blond
hair that begged to be touched, all of it coming together to form the quintessential fantasy. Rusty
couldn't remember ever being mesmerized like that.
There was no disputing the fact that the woman was
not merely attractive, but stunningly gorgeous by anyone's standards.

And he had a feeling that her looks had not come
without some heavy price tag. The woman had a chip
on her shoulder a mile wide and obviously didn't trust
people easily.

But then, he'd always been the patient one in his
family.

Without saying another word in his defense, Rusty
opened his wallet, flipping past the photographs he
had of his older brother and sister, of his mother and
the father they all rarely spoke of—the one who had
inadvertently been instrumental in getting all three of
them involved in the agency that tried to undo horrible wrongs done to children and their families. As
far as Rusty knew, he was the only member of the
family who actually had a picture of their late father,

although he knew that Chad had eventually made his peace with the man who had all but ruined his life.

He held the wallet open to show the woman the private investigator's license that had been issued to him a week after he'd graduated from the University of Bedford with his degree in criminology.

As he watched, a layer of the disbelief on her face melted away.

Score one for the home team, he thought.

Taking one of the business cards that Cade Townsend, the founder of the agency, had presented to him as a graduation gift, Rusty handed it to the woman. "This is where I work."

"'ChildFinders Inc.,'" she read out loud. "'Russell Andreini.'" Looking up, she held the card out to him. "You don't look like a Russell."

Rusty smiled. "Everyone says that."

For a while, when he'd been younger and taken himself more seriously, he'd tried to convince people to address him by his given name, but it just never took. Everyone kept forgetting. Eventually he stopped reminding them that his name was now Russell and resigned himself to being Rusty, the person people always opened up to. As time went on, he'd come to the conclusion that he wouldn't have it any other way.

He moved to close her hand over it, but she jerked it away. "Keep it."

She pursed her lips as she looked at the card again. The address was a street she wasn't familiar with, but then, she was new to the area. As she had been to the seven other areas she'd lived in these past two years.

Everyone, she thought, was always looking out for number one. "You're looking for a job."

What had happened to make her this cynical? he wondered. His sister Megan had always had a tart tongue, but there had never been this edge to it, this me-against-the-world attitude that he sensed within the woman he was talking to.

"I'm looking to help," he told her quietly.

Dakota looked down at the fancy writing on the card and ran her thumb over the raised letters. Expensive. She blew out a breath.

"Well, if this is on the level, I probably can't afford you," she said cynically.

Money was the last thing he was thinking of. "We're flexible. Something can be worked out."

She'd had men trying to find a way into her life and her bed since she was fourteen years old. That was when she'd reached her full height and had ripened. Her beauty had been more curse than blessing, until she had learned to make it work for her.

Her eyes hardened. "I'll bet."

He wasn't going to waste time arguing with her about his own motives. Instead, he gave her a little background information.

"Cade Townsend founded the agency when his own son was kidnapped. My sister was the FBI agent who worked the case. She joined him a couple of months after he opened his doors."

Dakota had a tendency to not believe what was told to her, or to at least take it with a huge grain of salt.

But there was something in Rusty's eyes...something that seemed sincere.

She hesitated. "Did they ever find his son?"

"Yeah, they did." The smile on his face fairly lit it up. "And a whole lot of other kids along the way. They're still finding them." He saw doubt war with something else in her eyes. This one wasn't easily convinced of anything. "You can look up anything you want about the agency on the Internet."

"I don't own a computer."

Her statement took him by surprise. His whole life revolved around technology and the answers it could yield. He'd gotten into it because of Megan, whose wizardry at the computer was outdone only and just marginally by that of Savannah King Walters, Sam's wife, who worked for them part-time. It had gotten so that Rusty assumed everyone had at least one computer in their lives, if not several. There was one in each room in his apartment.

"That makes you rather unique."

Dakota, decades weary beyond her twenty-four years, laughed dryly. "Right, unique."

She fingered the card Rusty had refused to take back, her mind working at a frantic pace. Nothing mattered but getting Vinny back. She thought she knew *who* had taken him, was pretty sure on that score, but she had no idea *where* he had been taken. There were at least several possibilities, if not more.

Even if she did know where, she knew she couldn't just waltz in and get Vinny. Not without help. Without backup. She looked at the man in front of her. Maybe she needed this overgrown Boy Scout at that.

But she wanted him to convince her, to make her feel that she wasn't going to regret this decision. "How good is your track record? Fifty percent? Sixty?" she added hopefully.

Rusty shook his head and her heart plummeted.

"Well, then, I guess I don't—"

"One hundred." He saw her eyes widen at the number. "Our track record is one hundred percent," he told her.

She knew it. It was a scam. All of it. She thrust the card at him, jabbing at a chest that was harder than she'd expected.

"You're lying," she accused angrily. Did he think she was some kind of mental midget? Nobody had that kind of success.

He merely looked down at the card she was pushing against him, but didn't take it from her.

"It's a matter of record. No case we take on is ever closed until we find the missing child. Sometimes we get lucky and it's fast, sometimes not, but we never give up." It was a promise he was making her. "It took three years to find Darin, Cade's son," he added when she looked at him blankly as he said the name.

Oh, God, she wanted to believe him so badly. But she'd stopped believing in Santa Claus the year she'd turned six. "How much does all this cost?" There was still some jewelry she could sell, she thought. Pieces Vincent had given her to convince her of the seriousness of his intentions. She'd been saving them for an emergency and this more than qualified.

"Like I said, things can be arranged. We're not in it for the money."

Next he was going to tell her that he was a monk in disguise. "But you've got to eat," she pointed out cynically. "And your apartment upstairs doesn't come free."

"We can take your case pro bono." He knew Cade would have no problem with that. Cade had been the one who had said that money was secondary to their work. His superior was completely dedicated to the belief that no one should be made to go through what he had.

"I don't need charity." Her indignation heated and then she looked past him toward the framed photograph on the coffee table. The photograph of her and Vinny taken on his last birthday. They'd been in Salinas then. Two locations ago. "What I need is my son back."

"I know you do. And we're going to do whatever's necessary to find him and get him back."

He hadn't used the word "try," she noted. It was almost as if he was making her a promise. God, she wished she could believe that he was on the level, wished that she wasn't so damn suspicious of everything and everyone.

But there was good reason to be.

The phone rang just then.

Dakota jumped. Her nerves all close to the surface,

she bit her lower lip to stifle the scream that had risen instantly.

But as she swung around and reached for the receiver, Rusty caught her wrist. She looked at him accusingly. Was he crazy?

"Tilt the receiver so I can listen in," he instructed.

She hated the fact that he seemed so matter-of-fact, so calm, while she felt as if she were on a giant roller coaster barreling down an incline. Dakota jerked her hand free just as he released his hold. Grabbing the phone with both hands, she cried, "Hello?" breathlessly.

There was a slight delay before a metallic voice asked, "Is this Della Armstrong?"

"Dakota," she corrected heatedly. Something was wrong. They knew her name. She didn't doubt that they knew everything about her. Was this supposed to be some kind of cryptic put-down?

"Sorry," the voice on the other end of the line said cheerfully. "Ms. Armstrong, this is Phil Henderson from Dayton Telemarketing. We're calling people in your neighborhood tonight to—"

She slammed down the receiver, swallowing a curse as angry tears filled her eyes. "Of all the stupid times to call..."

He heard the barely suppressed hysteria in her voice, knew where it could lead if unleashed. "Easy," Rusty cautioned.

Her temper exploded. "Easy, right. You can take it easy," she lashed out. "It's not your son who was stolen out of his crib."

She had every right to think that he didn't understand, but he did. More than she could ever know. He understood anguish. And hated it. "We'll find him."

"How do I know that?" she demanded hotly. "How do I know that Vinny won't be the blot on your sterling record? The one who you couldn't get back." She bit back a sob. "You have no right, no right to make promises you can't keep."

He took hold of her shoulders. She struggled to pull away but this time he wouldn't let her. This time, he held her fast. "Look at me."

Defiant, she refused to obey. She'd always resented being told what to do.

"Why?"

"Look at me," he repeated, measuring out each word. His tone surprised her. When she reluctantly did what he wanted, Rusty said in a firm voice, "Your son isn't going to be an exception. We are going to find him. You have to believe that."

She wanted to. He had no idea how much she wanted to. But she knew the odds, knew what he was up against even if he didn't. How could he?

Desperation made her cynical. "You and this boss of yours and your sister, the ex-FBI agent."

He refused to let her bait him, even though he sensed that she was after an argument, that a verbal fight might somehow alleviate the tension holding her prisoner. It wasn't in his nature to argue.

"There are more people working at the agency now," he assured her. "My brother—"

She didn't let him finish. Disgust came into her eyes. "What is this, a family affair?"

"In a way." In some ways, they were closer than some families. They agonized over each other's cases, shared each other's successes. "My brother was kidnapped as a boy, so I kind of know what you're going through. The others at the agency all have had close experiences with kidnap victims and their families. Nobody thinks of this as just another job, or any of the kids we look for as just statistics." This wasn't the time to go into any of that. He'd just wanted to reassure her a little. "Now, are you up to giving me some information, or do you want me to call someone to stay with you tonight and we'll talk in the morning at the agency?"

Morning. A million light-years from now. Where would Vinny be in the morning? Would he be calling for her? Would he be afraid? Or would they begin brainwashing him, making him forget her? How long did a two-year-old's memory last?

She was becoming aware of a numbness settling in. One that separated her from her body and her anguish, making things seem surreal. It crept slowly up her limbs. Maybe it was all a nightmare, a horrible, horrible nightmare. That was it, a nightmare. She'd lived in fear of this happening for two years, maybe it had just surfaced in a dream to haunt her.

"There's no one to call," she told him dully. There would have been if this had been her old life. There were people she could turn to. But not here. There was no one here.

Rusty thought of calling his sister, or Savannah, who'd come to work for the agency after Sam had recovered her daughter.

Elizabeth, another detective at the agency, might even be more suited to dealing with this woman, he realized, because of her pronounced sensitivity, but then he remembered that she was away on a case. Still, the woman needed someone to remain with her.

"If you want, I can—"

The dullness abated for a moment as alarms went off within her. She knew it. He was going to say he'd make the sacrifice and stay the night with her. He might be sweet-sounding, but in the end, all men were the same. They all had only one goal.

"No," she snapped. "You can't."

She was a grown woman. Granted, she was a woman in need, but he wasn't going to argue with her about staying with her. Maybe she would do better on her own. Everybody needed space at times.

"All right." He started for the door. "You know where to find me if you need me. I'll be upstairs after I look around."

She didn't understand. Her brain was becoming dull again, giving in to the numbness that was overtaking her. "You already looked around."

"That was just a fast scan, to see if there was anyone around. This time it'll be slower." Clues could be left in the oddest places and people always slipped up somewhere. "You never know what you can find."

The people she was up against were professionals.

They made it their life's work to not make mistakes. If the Boy Scout thought otherwise, he was wrong. Dakota began to say something, but the words somehow vanished from her lips.

As did the rest of the room less than a second after that.

Rusty caught her just in time to keep her from hitting the floor.

"Maybe you're not as tough as you think you are," he commented under his breath as he scooped her into his arms. Relaxed, the young woman's features lost their edginess. They were soft and she looked a lot younger. A lot more innocent.

As he looked at her, Rusty felt something within him stir and banked it down without examination. This wasn't the time or the place. She was a client even though she hadn't actually asked to retain his services. In any event, he couldn't think of her in any different terms until her situation was resolved.

Looking around, he decided to put her in her own bed rather than on the sofa. Entering the room, he made his way over to the bed and placed her on top of the comforter. He took one end of it and placed it over her. There was a chill in the air and he didn't want it bringing her around. She could do with a little rest. With any luck, she'd sleep until morning.

In the meantime, he had some work to do.

There was something heavy on her chest, pressing down hard, making it difficult for her to breathe.

As she struggled to rise above the haze encasing

her, Dakota slowly realized that the heavy weight wasn't on her chest, it was *in* her chest.

It was her heart.

It felt as if it weighed a thousand pounds. A thousand pounds and yet it was empty.

Vinny.

Oh, God, they'd taken Vinny. Her precious, sweet, innocent little boy. They'd taken him from her just the way she'd been afraid they would. Afraid for these past two years.

She'd been right to be afraid.

Her eyes were still shut tight even though she thought she'd already opened them. Twice.

With effort, Dakota forced her eyelids up. The haze seemed to cling to everything around her. She blinked twice, then focused on her surroundings.

She was in her bedroom. The edge of her comforter was partially thrown over her, as if she'd been tucked into bed.

When had she gone to bed?

She hadn't, she remembered. She'd been in the kitchen, trying to get rid of that man with the dimple in his cheek when everything had gone black.

The man with the dimple. The private investigator or baby finder or whatever he called himself.

What if he—

Dakota struggled to sit upright, propping herself up on weakened elbows. The world was still not as steady as she wanted it to be, swimming around a little as she lifted her head. She blinked again, trying to bring everything back into focus.

Daylight was trying to squeeze itself in through the blinds. What time was it? How long had she been lying here?

She turned her head to look at the digital clock on her nightstand when she saw him. Andreini, sitting in her rocking chair, the only piece of furniture in the furnished apartment that she'd bought herself, besides the crib.

His head drooped against his chest.

Had he been here all night?

She looked down at her nightgown to see if it was in place. Had he tried anything?

"I thought you'd be more comfortable in your own bed than on the sofa."

She jumped at the sound of his voice and upbraided herself for it. She was behaving like a spooked rabbit. "You're awake."

"Yes, I'm awake." He'd only shut his eyes a few minutes ago, giving in to fatigue. "I don't usually sound too coherent when I'm talking in my sleep. At least, so I've been told."

Dakota swung her legs over the side of the bed, tugging down the edge of her nightgown before it crept up too high. He surprised her by keeping his eyes on her face. But maybe that was a cover.

"What happened?"

"You fainted," he said simply.

"And what did you do?"

"I caught you."

He was playing innocent with her. It didn't wash. "And?"

"I put you to bed. Alone. I've got a fingerprint kit upstairs if you'd like to dust yourself to look for any telltale prints," he offered mildly. "State of the art. Megan won't let us use anything less. That's my sister," he added.

The ex-FBI agent, she remembered. Feeling slightly woozy, Dakota forced herself to get up from the bed. "That won't be necessary."

"Good." He was on his feet, watching her. Ready to catch her again if need be. "Does that mean you're starting to trust me?"

Pulling herself up, Dakota looked at him pointedly. "No."

Chapter 3

Rusty scrutinized her for a long moment. "Well, at least you're honest."

She liked the fact that he didn't look away when he spoke, that he looked her square in the eye.

If a man can look you straight in the eye, Dee, he's got nothing to hide, her father had told her a long time ago. *Either that,* her mother had added, *or he's a cold-blooded liar.* Andreini didn't look like a cold-blooded liar. But she'd hold off making any final judgments about him until there were more facts in. She knew the danger of jumping to conclusions too soon.

"Don't feel bad," she told him, "I don't trust many people. I find it's a lot less disappointing that way." She looked at him and noted the rumpled clothing. "Did you stay here all night?"

He'd thought about going upstairs to his apartment several times after he finished looking around outside, but somehow he just hadn't felt right about leaving her alone. He'd only stopped upstairs long enough to get his shoes.

"Yes."

She continued looking at him. People usually squirmed under scrutiny. He didn't. Which meant that he had nothing to hide. Or everything to hide. Which was it? "Why?" She wanted to know.

He ran his hand through his hair, smoothing it down a little. His neck felt stiff, as did his shoulders. He'd never managed to develop his brother-in-law's trick of being able to catnap comfortably any place that came in handy. But he figured that was all part of Garret's Justice Department agent training.

"I wanted to be sure you were all right," he told her simply. "And I wanted to be here in case the kidnapper called." He saw her raise a brow, silently asking. "He didn't."

Had that been a slip? Was Andreini connected to the kidnapping after all? She wished she could stop vacillating and know one way or another. "How do you know it was a he?"

She'd asked the question rather heatedly, he noted, wondering why. "Print outside your window's too big for a woman."

"Print?" she echoed. "Just one?"

He nodded. The print would probably harden by mid-afternoon. Even though it was December, the Southern California sun could get pretty intense in the middle of the day. He'd have someone make a mold of it, or do it himself if there was no one available.

"It was a misstep. Whoever it was who took your son must have slid off the bridge and stepped into the dirt as he was leaving. Odds are that your son was probably taken not long after the sprinkler system went through its cycle." The sprinklers were timed and for some reason, management thought it best to have them go off at night rather than early morning. "The ground was still wet and he left a print." Because for once she seemed to be taking in what he was saying, Rusty told her the rest of what he'd discovered. "The sneaker's old. The heel is worn down on the side."

She pressed her lips together. "I guess maybe you really are a detective."

He grinned at her remark. "That's what I'd like to think."

The grin gave him an innocent, boyish quality. She wondered if he'd practiced it to make people let their guard down, or if it came naturally.

"Is there a trail?" Dakota knew it was foolish to hope that there was. The people she was dealing with didn't make mistakes. But even so, they were human. Maybe...

The next moment her heart sank as Andreini shook his head. She told herself it wasn't anything she hadn't expected.

"Just to the parking lot. Small flecks of mud on the asphalt," he explained. They had led to an empty carport. The kidnapper had probably parked there, taking a chance that the person the spot belonged to wouldn't come home to create a commotion about having someone in his or her space. "Even after I have it analyzed, I probably won't be sure if it came from the same sole, just from the same source, which is only logical."

Dakota frowned impatiently. She didn't want logic, she wanted her son.

"So where does that put us?" Back to square one, she thought before he could reply.

The key was to keep moving forward. Things had a way of happening when you kept them in motion. "In my office, asking questions."

She looked at him suspiciously. "What kind of questions?"

There was that wary tone again. What was she afraid he'd find out? What was she hiding? "Hopefully helpful ones. The more I know about your son, his routine—"

She felt her patience fraying again, just as it had last night. "He's two years old, he doesn't have a routine."

"Everyone has a routine," he corrected. "Even if it's only one that's imposed on a child by his mother. The more I know," Rusty repeated, "the better equipped I am to find him quickly."

There was that assurance again. No hesitation, just a tacitly understood guarantee. She'd lived long enough in Las Vegas to know that there was no such thing as a guarantee or a sure thing. Only fools who believed in them. Andreini sounded confident, as confident as a greenhorn watching his first spin of the roulette wheel.

Yet he didn't really strike her as being a fool, or gullible.

Dakota bit her lip. She knew that she was hoping for the impossible—that somehow this man who'd pushed his way into her life was right. That he would get Vinny back for her. Quickly, before the man who had him taken could make her son forget her.

God, but she hated being this vulnerable, this easy a target emotionally. Self-conscious, she glanced down and realized that she'd slept in the sweater she'd dragged on last night to cover up.

She had to look as bad as she felt. ''I need a shower and to put on some clothes.''

The latter was a matter of opinion, Rusty thought, but he wasn't about to say that out loud. As far as he was concerned, the woman in front of him looked great just the way she was, with the mark of sleep still in her eyes and her hair all mussed and tangled, fresh from her bed.

Maybe he could do with a shower himself, Rusty thought. A cold one. The hot one he'd been planning on to get the stiffness out of his shoulders would have to be temporarily put on hold.

''Me, too,'' he agreed. ''I'll be back within an hour.'' That should give her enough time, he judged. ''We can do the interview here if you want. That way, if a ransom call does come, you'll be here to get it.''

But she shook her head at his offer. Though she'd jumped when the telephone had rung last night, she wasn't expecting to receive any calls. Not if Vinny had been taken by the person she suspected. The man didn't want to contact her. There was nothing she could offer in exchange for her son, nothing he wanted *but* her son.

"I don't have to be here," she told him. "I can have the calls forwarded to my cell phone," she added as an afterthought.

Dakota led the way out of her room. "Besides, I'd rather go down to your office."

He was coming to understand the way her mind worked. She took nothing at face value. "To see if it's on the level?"

The barest hint of a smile curved her mouth. "Something like that."

Rusty nodded. He preferred it that way, actually. It certainly wouldn't hurt to have her see the framed photographs of the children they'd recovered. The extensive gallery covered the length of one complete wall and was designed to inspire hope in every despairing parent who crossed their threshold. He figured it would do the same for her.

"Want me to pick you up?" He knew the answer to that even before the words were out of his mouth.

She crossed to her front door and opened it. "No, I can find my own way."

He merely nodded, accepting her need for independence. Everyone found their own way to deal with a tragedy. She was a hell of a lot stronger than most of the women he'd encountered who had been in her place.

Walking out of the apartment, he turned around abruptly. "One more thing."

About to close the door, she looked up impatiently. "What?"

"Your name." She'd never once introduced herself. "Did I hear you correctly last night?"

That's right, she realized, she'd avoided telling him her name, but he'd heard her correcting the telemarketing person who'd called last night. That had been a slip. Maybe her mistake was in not having changed it, but that had been because she'd believed that the man who had taken her son only knew her by her stage name. It had given her a sense of security, of comfort, to revert to her own name.

Showed what she knew, she thought contemptuously.

Dakota left her hand on the door. "Depends on what you think you heard."

Cagey, always cagey. It was beginning to fascinate him. "Dakota Armstrong."

She gave a slight nod. "That's me."

Somehow, although he had no idea what a Dakota Armstrong would look like, the name suited her. It was different, unique. As was she.

Rusty put out his hand. "Glad to know you, Dakota Armstrong."

She didn't take his hand. She didn't want a friend, she wanted someone who could do something for her. So instead, she merely closed the door on him.

Her voice came through the barrier. "I'll see you in about an hour."

Shaking his head, Rusty hurried up the stairs to his apartment.

He made it to his office in almost half that time. A five-minute shower was all he'd needed before he'd hurried into a fresh pair of jeans and a new shirt. He let the wind dry his hair as he drove to the office, leaving the top down on the vintage blue-and-white Mustang convertible that Megan and Chad had given him for graduation. It was the car he'd spent the better part of two years fantasizing about when he hadn't been immersed in the minutia of forensics.

He'd expected to be the first one in the office. He'd expected wrong.

There was no need to insert the key into the lock. The door wasn't locked. As he turned the knob and walked in, he saw Megan coming out of the coffee room, a mug of coffee in one hand, a plate containing two-thirds of a Danish pastry in the other.

Her expression immediately brightened when she saw him. "Hello, little brother, what brings you in so early?" She temporarily set down both mug and plate on the desk in the middle of the foyer. Carrie, their secretary, wasn't due for another hour. "I thought you'd be basking in your success and sleeping in today." Before he could respond, she added, "Mrs. Quinn left a message on the machine this morning, saying that she just wanted you to know that there'll always be a place set for you at their table."

He'd almost forgotten about yesterday. He'd found the Quinns's eight-year-old daughter earlier that morning. One of the informants Ben—another partner at the agency who'd come to them via the police department—had cultivated during his career had tipped them off about a little girl who fit Julie Quinn's description being held in a nearby vacant warehouse. Rescue and reunion had taken place in a matter of hours.

Rusty shrugged. Gratitude always made him feel awkward, like someone who'd suddenly become too big for his clothes. ''Place setting belongs to Ben as much as to me.''

''That's my little brother, modest to a fault.'' Affection entered her eyes as Megan reached up and patted his face. She left her hand where it was as she studied him. Had he been up all night?

''You look tired, Rusty. Why *didn't* you sleep in?''

He grinned as he took her hand in his and removed it. ''You're being a mother again.''

''Sorry, habit.''

He knew she wasn't alluding to the fact that she had a child of her own these days. The habit had been ingrained in her long before then. Megan had been more like a mother than a sister to him while he was growing up. Their own mother had slowly shrunk away from reality, retreating into a world of her own making after Chad had been kidnapped, until she all but disappeared. Discovering two years later that her ex-husband had been the one to kidnap their son had done nothing to stabilize her world. So, Megan, still a child herself, had taken over being both parents as well as sibling to him. He'd never felt himself short-changed, not even once. There wasn't anything he wasn't willing to do for Megan. Where it might have divided some, the crisis had only succeeded in bringing them closer.

Megan held herself in check, squelching the desire to tell him to turn around and go home. "But you're still not answering my question."

He knew she'd keep after him until he told her. Megan hated not knowing anything. "Client coming in this morning."

News to her. Cade hadn't said anything about a new client coming to the office. Which meant that he didn't know. "You're drumming up business in the street these days?" she asked Rusty.

"It's my neighbor," he told her. "Two-year-old was kidnapped last night sometime between eight and eleven. Stolen right out of his bedroom."

Though she was juggling two cases at the moment, Megan's interest was instantly aroused. "Do the police have any leads?"

"They weren't called in." He saw surprise register on his sister's face. "Client didn't want them." And, whenever possible, they tried to adhere to the client's wishes.

"Why not?"

He shrugged. She wasn't asking anything that he hadn't asked himself. "My guess is that the client's running away from something."

"Sounds like something caught up." Megan picked up her mug and plate again. There were files waiting to be reviewed on her computer. "You going to need help?"

The offer wasn't unexpected. They all shared time on each other's cases. But somehow, when it came from his sister, he found himself chafing just the slightest bit. "I'll know where to find you if I do." He paused, then added, "I know how to ride a two-wheeler by myself now, Megan."

He was referring to the time she'd taught him how to ride a bicycle. His coordination had been less than stellar in those days and he'd crashed a dozen times or so before finally getting the hang of it. She knew he was telling her to back off in polite terms. But she hadn't made the offer because she didn't think he could handle the job, she'd made it because she liked helping.

"Right." Standing on her toes, Megan managed to reach his cheek and brushed a kiss on it. "I'm never going to get used to the idea that somebody whose bottom I diapered is now taller than I am."

"A foot taller," he emphasized. "And I'd just as soon you deep-sixed the diaper story if you don't mind."

It was all the heads-up Megan needed. She laughed. "Widowed or divorced?"

Rusty looked at his sister with complete innocence. "Who?"

He wasn't fooling her for a second. "The woman who's coming in."

"What makes you think it's a woman?" He'd deliberately used the word client.

Megan grinned, forgetting her queasy stomach for the moment. "The FBI isn't in the habit of hiring dummies."

"Just nosy women," he teased. He eyed the partially consumed pastry on her plate. It reminded him that he'd completely forgotten about breakfast this morning. Until now. "You going to eat that?"

She pushed the paper plate toward him. "Be my guest. My stomach isn't feeling quite up to par this morning. I don't know why I even bothered buying that."

Now that he thought of it, whenever he'd seen her this past week, Megan had looked rather pale. Rusty raised a brow just as he heard the door open behind him. "You're not...?"

Megan knew exactly what he was thinking. Because it had been in the back of her mind for the past seven days. Ever since she'd thrown up.

"Not that I know of." She gave him a warning look as she cut him off. The last thing she wanted was to have rumors flying around the office before she was sure there was a reason for them.

But it was too late. Sam Walters had come into the office with his wife, Savannah. Overhearing enough to piece together the rest, he came over and draped an arm over Megan's shoulder. He and Megan went way back, to the days when he'd been on the police force and she'd been a rookie special agent.

"Another little Wichita on the way, huh? Maybe we should seriously think about opening up a nursery on the side. Certainly make a nice statement about the place.'' He looked at Megan. ''So, what do you want this time, a boy or a girl?''

''What I want,'' Megan said, retreating into her own office, ''is some peace and quiet so I can finally wrap up the paperwork on my last case.''

''Holler if you need anything,'' Rusty called after her. He grinned, taking a bite of the Danish she'd surrendered as she pretended to give him a reproachful look.

''Likewise,'' she echoed, closing her door.

He finished the pastry before he ever reached his office. The sound of the front door opening again caught his attention a second before he crossed the threshold. Turning, he saw Dakota walk into the main office.

Because Carrie hadn't yet arrived, Savannah greeted the statuesque blonde, silently wishing she had the other woman's figure. She was trim and athletic, but curves like those of the woman in the powder-blue suit were to be envied.

''May I help you?''

Dakota looked around before answering and saw Rusty. She pointed toward him. ''I'm here to see him.''

Standing next to his wife, Sam said, ''Lucky him,'' in a voice audible only to Savannah. She gave him a jab in the ribs with her elbow and he laughed. ''I'll behave,'' he promised, giving her an affectionate nuzzle. ''God knows you're woman enough for me.''

''And don't you forget it,'' Savannah told him,

managing to keep a straight face until after he'd entered his own office.

Dakota caught the tail end of the exchange and felt a fleeting tinge of envy. She'd never enjoyed that sort of relationship with a man, the kind that came with lighthearted teasing and heavy doses of love. Not even with Vincent.

"I was hoping you wouldn't change your mind," Rusty told her as he waited for her to enter his office.

"Why?"

"Because I want to help."

She could almost believe him. He sounded sincere. But she knew the only reason he wanted to help, no matter what he said, was because of the money. What she had in her purse would more than cover any fee he wanted to charge.

"Have a seat." Rusty gestured to the chair in front of his desk. He closed the door behind her before crossing to his own chair, then waited until she sat before beginning. She looked not unlike a bird on a wire, trying her best to not lose her balance. "Change your mind about going to the police?"

"No." The retort was immediate and sharp. Her voice softened a shade. "I haven't. I told you before, I don't want the police brought in on this."

She'd seemed genuinely concerned about her son. Why was she so wary of the police? *Had* the kidnapper contacted her and issued the standard threat about killing the hostage if the police were summoned? She had to know the police were still her first, best bet. "Do you mind telling me why?"

She never flinched as she returned his gaze. "Yes, I do mind."

Kidnappings were hard enough without facing obstacles provided by the parent. "I can't help you if you keep things back."

There was no way to read the look in her eyes. "What about that track record you were bragging about?"

If they were going to get anywhere, she was going to have to get rid of that chip on her shoulder. He tried diplomacy. "Most parents are completely open with us, telling us everything they can in order to help us find their missing children."

She looked down at her perfectly lacquered nails, torn. Consumed with worry. She wasn't afraid for Vinny's safety, she was just afraid of never seeing him again. "What is it you want to know?"

He began with the logical question, taking out the tape recorder he kept in his desk. Cade had few rules, but one of them was that the first interview had to be taped. "Would Vinny's father kidnap his son? Or have him kidnapped?"

The question passed by her, unheard. She was staring at the tape recorder. "What are you doing?"

She was acting as if he'd put a snake on the table instead of a machine, Rusty thought. "Taping the conversation."

"Why?" It was a demand, not a question.

"Agency rules. Just a way to keep the facts fresh and on record."

She wanted to tell him to put it away. She wanted

to bolt. But most of all, she wanted Vinny. So she didn't tell him to get rid of the machine and she didn't leave. Folding her hands in front of her, exercising extreme control over her worn nerve endings, she looked at him.

"What did you ask me?"

Rusty repeated the question. "Would Vinny's father kidnap his son? Or have him kidnapped?"

"No."

In his estimation, she'd answered too emphatically. "No disrespect, but maybe you don't know the man as well as you think you do—"

Dakota laughed shortly. He had that right. "Truer words were never said, Andreini, but even so, I know he wasn't the one to take the boy."

He had to push it to the limit. There was more than one case of a child taken by an estranged spouse in their files. "What makes you so sure?"

She set her mouth grimly. "Because Vinny's father is dead." And that was when the trouble had all started, she remembered.

"Oh." He couldn't gauge by her tone whether the man's death had left her bereft or relieved. "I'm sorry."

She lifted her shoulders carelessly, not about to display any more emotion in front of this stranger than she already had. "Yeah, so am I. He had a lot of faults, but he was a good guy. Or tried to be," she amended, saying it more to herself than to Rusty.

There was a hell of a lot more to this than she was

telling him, Rusty thought. He had to get her to talk to him. And for that, he was going to have to get her to trust him.

He figured he had his work cut out for him.

Chapter 4

Making himself comfortable, Rusty took out the worn notepad he kept in his pocket, the one that seemed to have an endless supply of paper and had been with him since he'd started. If he had one superstition, he would have had to say it revolved around the notepad. Every case he'd entered there had been solved.

"Let's start with where you work."

"Why?"

It certainly hadn't taken long for her defensiveness to kick in again. He'd hoped that maybe she would have put it aside once they'd actually gotten started.

"Because I intend to go there and scout around, maybe talk to a few people."

She didn't want him talking to the people she worked with, didn't want any suspicions being raised.

It was her business that this was happening, not anyone else's.

"There's no reason for that," she protested. "Vinny was stolen out of his crib in the apartment, not out of a dressing room."

He wasn't sure just what she was alluding to. Maybe she worked at a clothing shop. The one thing he did know was that he had to get her to be more cooperative or this investigation wasn't going to go anywhere. The woman had to be convinced of the validity of every step he took and to stop challenging each one as it occurred, otherwise this wasn't going to go anywhere.

Maybe a little personal insight would help. He knew Sam and Savannah wouldn't mind.

"The woman you passed earlier is Savannah Walters. Her little girl was kidnapped by the wife of someone she worked with at the time of the abduction. Someone she trusted," he emphasized. He leaned forward, making his point as sincerely as he could. "I need to talk to anyone you've had contact with to rule out that possibility."

Resistance came naturally to her. She'd been resisting for so long that it was second nature to her. "I can rule it out for you right now. I'm not that friendly with anyone at work."

"Why doesn't that surprise me?" he said under his breath as he jotted something down on his pad.

She raised a brow, immediately on the defensive. "What?"

That had been a slip. It wasn't like him. Rusty admonished himself as he looked up. "You seem like the private type."

Dakota frowned slightly. That wasn't what he'd said originally. "I believe in minding my own business."

"I still need your place of business." He indicated an empty line on the form. "For the record. Humor me," he told her when she didn't respond.

With a sigh, she gave him the address of the store where she worked in Newport Beach. It didn't matter really. As soon as she got Vinny back, Dakota already knew she'd be clearing out. Maybe even leaving the country this time, although she hated the thought of doing something that drastic. But to keep her son safe, she was willing to do anything, to go to any lengths. Nothing meant anything to her without Vinny.

Rusty looked down at the name and address he'd just jotted down.

"Neiman-Marcus department store." It was a store he considered too expensive for even window-shopping. The one in Newport Beach had three stories. "That's a lot of people to not talk to." His expression was affable as he asked, "What do you do there?"

"I'm in sales." It wasn't what she'd wanted to do with her life, but it was the best she could get under the circumstances. Thinking that he probably thought the job beneath him, she added, "The position of Philosopher King was taken."

Rusty was surprised at the Aristotelian reference. He didn't take Dakota for someone who read such dry material. It had put him to sleep that one semester in college. "Don't you mean Philosopher Queen?"

"No," she contradicted. "King. A king's higher." Her mouth curved just the slightest bit. "I always aim for the best."

He didn't doubt it for a moment. She'd struck him as a class act the moment he'd seen her, someone who was accustomed to, and who got, the best. Which had made him wonder what she'd been doing living in his complex. It was a pleasant enough place in which to live and the surrounding area was nice, but there was nothing upper echelon about it. And neither was there about the job she had. Yet she read or at least was familiar with Aristotle. The woman was an enigma.

Rusty moved on to the next item. "I'll also need a list of friends."

Her eyes narrowed almost imperceptibly. "Don't you have any of your own?"

She was sharper-tongued and less frantic than she had been last night or even this morning. Had the kidnapper contacted her? And if so, why wasn't she saying anything?

"Mine won't help, yours might," he said dryly.

There weren't any friends, not here. She couldn't allow herself to get close to anyone anymore. The woman at the day-care center where she left Vinny had tried more than once to get her to open up, or at least to get together with some of the other mothers, but she had steadfastly remained distant. It was safer that way.

"I told you, I'm a private person."

His expression was innocent as he studied her. "No friends?"

"No need."

It was a lie. She had a very real need to share, to lean, and there were friends, but they were all back in Las Vegas and she couldn't risk contacting any of them. It was like being in the witness protection program without the comfort of safety.

Rusty didn't buy that answer, either. No one was an island, even if they thought they were. Because of what he'd gone through, his brother Chad had been distant, like Dakota, but even Chad had eventually recognized his own need for contact, for warmth. Rusty reasoned that it would be the same for Dakota.

"Has there been anyone you noticed hanging around in the area lately? Anyone unusual?"

One side of her mouth raised a fraction of an inch as she looked at him. "You mean, other than you?"

She was referring to the times he had tried to get a conversation going with her. "I live there, remember?"

The hint of a smile faded and she shook her head. "No, no one unusual."

He looked at her steadily. "And no one's contacted you?"

Her impatience surfaced again. "I already told you they hadn't."

Rusty sighed inwardly. He felt like a lawyer with a hostile witness on the stand. It wasn't usually like this. Most of the time the parent was only too eager to keep talking, hoping that something would lead to their child's recovery. Doggedly, he pressed on.

As he continued asking questions, he noted that Dakota vacillated between being wary, snappish and wry. Writing down her answers in his own brand of shorthand, Rusty continued to wonder why she would behave in such a fashion, considering the circumstances.

He had no way of knowing that the woman sitting so rigidly in front of him was wrestling with her thoughts and her conscience. Throughout the questioning, she kept trying to decide whether or not to be completely honest and tell Rusty who she believed had abducted her son. But each qualm of conscience brought fear with it. Fear that if Rusty knew who he might be facing, he would back away. And she did need him.

But not telling him might delay finding Vinny. In addition, keeping Andreini in the dark might also prove dangerous to him, if not fatal.

The man had a right to know who he was up against.

But, she insisted silently, she had a right to get back her son.

Dakota played with the tips of her nails and decided, for the time being, to keep silent about the identity of the man who'd cast such a dark shadow over her life for the past two years.

Half an hour later, she saw Rusty close his notepad and hit the stop button on the tape recorder. For now, the questions stopped.

She had a question of her own.

"You haven't talked about payment."

He'd never been good when it came to talking about money. As a teenager, because he had always been naturally handy, he had worked on neighbors' cars to earn spending money. But he had always had trouble asking for what was due him. Exasperated when she thought people were taking advantage of him, Megan had taken over the financial end of his business.

"You can stop at Carrie's desk on your way out, she'll be happy to go over everything with you. If there's any problem," he said, anticipating that there would be strictly because of what she'd said in her apartment last night, "it can be worked out. The main thing is to find your son."

She was starting to believe that *he* believed that. "Yes, it is, but I don't intend to do that on credit."

Dakota dug into her purse, searching for what she'd slipped inside just before she'd left. Her fingers curved around the multifaceted surfaces.

She tossed the item on his desk with a carelessness that surprised him. He'd thought that every woman revered jewelry. The diamond necklace sitting on top of his papers would have inspired reverence in a Spartan.

The sparkle emanating from it was almost blinding. "Is it real?"

"As real as you are." She tried to not think about

when she had received it from Vincent. He'd made her close her eyes before he'd slipped it around her neck. She'd felt like a queen. She'd felt loved. What she'd been, she knew, was blinded. She smiled at Rusty. "I never accept imitations."

The smile struck him as incredibly sad. Rusty picked up the long, gleaming string of near-perfect diamonds. When the sunlight hit it, it was like holding blue fire with his fingertips. He couldn't begin to estimate its worth.

"I don't think the bill's going to be quite this high."

She shrugged carelessly. The necklace had been in its box since Vincent had died. Because she'd accidentally discovered the necklace's true origin, the gift no longer meant anything to her. He'd bought it for someone else, but had taken it back after the breakup.

"Make change," she told him, rising.

"Two bracelets and a pair of earrings?" he offered, raising a brow.

"Whatever." She didn't care about the necklace. She cared about getting Vinny back. Quickly. Dakota paused in the doorway. "You'll call me if there's anything?"

He crossed to the doorway to stand beside her. Who had been the man in her life? Did she miss him? Had she hardened her heart to everyone because losing him had been so devastating? Questions occurred to him that weren't restricted to the immediate case at hand. He wanted them answered.

"I'll call you regularly one way or another."

She only wanted to hear from him if he had something positive to tell her. She didn't know how much more of this she could take without breaking. "Make it one way," she instructed.

She left Rusty standing with the necklace still in his hand and myriad questions preying on his mind.

"Can't say much about her." The thin, aristocratic-looking bald man mopped his head before stuffing his handkerchief back into his jacket pocket. The overhead light in his cubicle seemed designed to make him perspire despite the temperature in the rest of the department store.

"She does her work well enough," Seth Masterson continued. He gave Rusty the feeling that he was testing out each word in his head before saying it out loud. "Not a real go-getter, like some who work here, but customers seem to think she knows what she's talking about because she's so attractive."

A wispy smile crossed his lips. In Rusty's judgment the man almost sounded as if he had some sort of a crush on Dakota. He made a mental note of the man's name. Maybe Masterson'd taken Vinny to secure Dakota's love. Stranger things happened.

"Half the women who shop here probably hope that they can wind up looking like her if they just use the right kind of makeup and buy the right kind of clothes." The department manager stopped, reconsidered his words. He leaned forward, lowering his voice. "Maybe I shouldn't have said that. That didn't sound sexist, did it?" He nibbled his near-nonexistent lower lip nervously. "They've got me going to one sensitivity program after another, and it's gotten so I'm afraid to say good morning to someone for fear they might read something into it that I never intended." He mopped his brow again, shaking his head mournfully. "Whole different world than when I first got started in retail."

Rusty nodded, doing his best to look sympathetic. He wasn't here to discuss the man's inability to adapt to the changing times. "How long has she worked for you?"

"For me?" The phrasing made Masterson smile again as he savored the notion. He didn't bother looking down at the sheet of paper in front of him. "Been here only six weeks. Little boy kidnapped you say, huh?" He shook his head. "I didn't even know she had a little boy." This time, he did glance at the form within the thin file he was holding. He ran his index finger over a space. "Yes, here it is under Dependents. She never talks about him. Never really talks at all," he amended. "Except to the customers."

Rusty leaned forward over the desk. He indicated the form. "Mind if I see that?"

Masterson hesitated, obviously debating the political correctness of sharing the information. He didn't appear inclined to hand over the form.

Rusty looked at him pointedly. "It might help me find her son."

Masterson debated a moment longer before surrendering the document.

"I don't see how, but knock yourself out—" And

then self-preservation kicked up another notch. "Just don't mention this to anyone, all right? I'm not sure about policy…"

"No problem," Rusty promised, taking the sheet from him. Blessed with a healthy ability to recall whatever he read, he perused the data quickly. What was on the form made him pause. Dakota had listed seven different addresses in seven different cities over the past two years. She was obviously on the run from something. "Moves around a bit, doesn't she?"

Masterson looked pleased at the observation. "That's exactly what I said to her. She told me she was looking for someplace that felt like home. Don't see anything wrong with that."

"No, nothing wrong with that," Rusty replied absently. "Just seems a little curious."

Her point of origin, he noted, was Las Vegas. At least, it had been two years ago. She hadn't mentioned that to him. Probably thought it was unimportant, he reasoned. He found himself wondering what kind of work she'd done in Vegas. He looked, but for some reason that had been left out of the report.

He'd looked for the department manager after talking to several other saleswomen on the floor. None of the conversations had yielded anything, except to prove that Dakota hadn't lied to him earlier. She wasn't close to anyone she worked with.

It was time to try another avenue. He handed the form back to the manager.

Masterson rose to his feet as soon as Rusty did. "Tell Ms. Armstrong that she doesn't have to come in tomorrow. Jackie'll cover for her.'' He nodded toward a small woman behind the register in the evening wear section. ''And that we all hope you find her little boy.''

''She'll appreciate that,'' Rusty told him, pocketing his notepad.

And he would appreciate a few more answers, Rusty thought, leaving the store.

She was going out of her mind.

She was just no good at waiting, no good at being patient. She *wasn't* patient by nature—at least, not with anyone but Vinny. With him she could be infinitely patient. She had to be. Vinny was pure charged energy and rarely seemed to be tired. He filled up all her hours at home to the point that she usually collapsed just after she put him to bed.

That was probably why she hadn't heard anything the night he was kidnapped, she thought, upbraiding herself. She'd probably dozed off without realizing it and been dead to the world.

Angry, she paced the length of the small living room again.

Maybe she should just take a plane to Vegas and confront the bastard.

But what if he wasn't on his estate? He liked to travel and there were a number of places the man could be. Vincent had once even told her that there was a family villa in Italy. Not to mention that there was a house in Chicago and a town house in New York. He could be in any one of a number of places.

With her son.

Emotions rushed up at her, battering her from all sides. She bit her lip, determined to not cry despite the overwhelming urge to do just that. Crying wasn't going to solve anything. It wasn't going to get Vinny back.

But she felt so damn alone. And so damn scared—

The sound of the doorbell made her jump nearly an inch off the floor. What if that was the kidnapper, back to do away with her? She wouldn't put it past the bastard to contract a hit on her now that he had what he wanted. That was his style. That was why Vincent had tried so hard to break away.

Looking for a weapon, she grabbed a steak knife from the sink and tucked it up inside the sleeve of her sweater. She could feel the comforting presence of the blade flat against her skin as she opened the door.

At first she was relieved, but relief was quickly followed by disappointment.

He was alone.

"It's you." A flicker of hope had her searching Rusty's face. "You didn't—"

Rusty shook his head. "No, I haven't found him." Not waiting for an invitation, he walked into the apartment.

"Well, nobody's called." She continued holding the door open, thinking he was going to leave. "Why are you here?"

He turned and, to her surprise, closed the door for her. "I've got more questions."

She blew out a breath. She didn't know how much more of this she could stand and still remain civil. "Questions aren't going to find my son."

He wasn't about to be outmaneuvered. "No, but answers might." He pinned her with a look, meaning to get at at least some of the truth. "Like, why you don't stay in one place for long."

He was supposed to be looking into finding her son, not into her past. "How did you—"

He wasn't about to be sidetracked. "Answer my questions first."

She shrugged, looking away. "I get bored easily. And I like to travel." Dakota raised her eyes to his face. Men loved it when you made them the center of your universe. "Let's just say I'm looking for the perfect fit."

Though she'd said the last sentence in a studied, seductive tone, he wasn't buying what she was selling. The seductress didn't ring any truer for him than the salesgirl did. There was more to this woman than was at first apparent. It was clear that she was a lady on the run with a secret, a secret that might or might not be directly related to her son's kidnapping.

"Let's just say you're lying," he contradicted, "and get that out of the way."

The best defense was an offense. She took immediate umbrage at his assumption. Nobody talked that way to her—even if it was true. "Hey—"

He cut her off. "Look, personally, it doesn't matter to me if you move every day and hit three hundred and sixty-five cities in a year, but whatever you're hiding or running from might have a direct impact on why your son was kidnapped and by whom. If you don't level with me,'' he told her again, ''I'm not going to be able to help you. The choice is yours.''

He was right. Or maybe he was just clever at wording things. Dakota resumed pacing, running her hands along her arms. She felt cold again.

When she swung around, it was to challenge him. ''How do I know I can trust you?''

For all she knew, he could be a plant. The organization had a great many tentacles, she'd discovered, and they could all reach far.

''I could show you my Boy Scout merit badge.'' And then Rusty's smile faded. He could give her references, but he knew she would distrust them, as well. Everything could be faked. ''You're going to have to start to trust somebody.''

If he only knew how ironic that sounded. That had been how everything had begun. Because she'd trusted. Trusted Vincent to not lie to her.

But he had.

Because he'd been afraid of losing her, he'd told her, pleading for her to understand. But it had been a lie all the same. A lie that had gotten her entrenched in deception and brought her to where she was today. A fugitive.

''I suppose you're right.'' She took a deep breath. ''All right, I'll level with you. I don't need you to run your investigation for me.'' The uncertainty she'd had last night about Vinny's abductors had been rooted in denial. She wasn't denying it any longer. "I need you for protection."

He waited for her to start making sense. "Go on."

She moistened her lips. This sounded so damn melodramatic, she thought, like something out of a script. But it was all true. "I need you to help me steal my son back."

"Then you do know who has him." He'd had a feeling all along that she had.

She nodded. "I think so."

The pieces fell into place. He'd seen the pattern before, though then it had been in a textbook. Being confronted with it in person put a whole different feel to it.

"Look, Ms. Armstrong, if this is some kind of a custody battle, you need a lawyer, not me."

"No," Dakota insisted, "I need you."

She heard the pleading note in her own voice and stifled it, ashamed of herself.

If not him, then someone else. It was just that he was already here and he might as well stay. There was something sympathetic about his eyes. Sympathetic and soft.

"Or, more accurately put, what I need is a hero." She turned on all the considerable charm she possessed inherently and had cultivated on the runway. "Will you be my hero, Andreini?"

Chapter 5

He looked at her for a long moment without answering. "That depends," Rusty said evenly, curbing an exuberance that came naturally to him and remembering Megan's edict about always looking before he leaped. Although, in his estimation, the red-blooded American male who wouldn't have leaped at the chance to be this woman's hero had probably been dead for about three or four days.

The cautious reply wasn't quite the answer she'd expected. Men had always been quick to do things for her, mistakenly thinking it was the fastest way to get her into bed. It pleased her that he wasn't like that, even though it miffed her a little at the same time.

Her eyes held his. "On what?"

Rusty met her scrutiny head-on. ''On whether or not you'll tell me the truth.''

Dakota took a deep breath, as if to fortify herself for the ordeal ahead, and then abruptly asked, ''Have you had dinner yet?''

Dinner. When had he last really had dinner? Since he'd joined the agency, his meals had consisted mostly of sandwiches or things tucked away in fast-food containers. Even before he'd been officially hired, he'd apprenticed with ChildFinders, giving them whatever free time he had whenever he wasn't on the U.C. Bedford campus. Mealtimes had fared no better then. Half the time he'd been too busy to stop to eat. As a happy side effect, the baby fat that had stubbornly remained with him through his early teen years had completely disappeared, replaced by lean muscle. He was now something he'd once heard called ''fighting trim.''

He shook his head in answer to her question, thinking it a put-off. ''No, but—''

Neither had she. She'd been too upset, too nervous, too angry to eat. Her last meal had been with Vinny last night. The vague notion that she should be trying to keep her strength up played through her head. ''How do you feel about salad?''

She was already turning toward her kitchen as she asked.

''Rabbit food,'' Chad called it. Rusty tended to agree, although he shrugged indifferently for Dakota's benefit. ''Never harbored any real feelings for salad one way or another. If it's in front of me, I'll eat it, but it's not something I make any effort to get.''

His answer amused her. ''Didn't mean for you to launch into a philosophical analysis.'' She opened the refrigerator. It was empty except for a couple of cans of diet soda, a bottle of water and a huge salad bowl covered with plastic wrap. She was to have gone to the store today, before everything had fallen apart on her. ''I keep a big bowl in the refrigerator. That way, I don't have to stop to prepare anything for me if I don't feel like it.''

Meals for Vinny were another matter. For him, she always prepared fresh meals, no leftovers for her boy. What was he eating tonight? She felt a sudden hitch in her throat.

Rusty could think of a great many things that were more appetizing than salad. ''I could take you out to dinner.''

She was in the process of removing two small bowls from the overhead cupboard. He tried not to notice the way her short sweater crept up on her taut, toned stomach as she reached. It wasn't easy keeping his thoughts confined.

''You could,'' she allowed, setting the bowls down on the countertop. ''If I let you.''

He picked up on her meaning immediately. She thought he was hitting on her. ''It wouldn't be a date.''

On second thought, she decided, he was too straightforward for that kind of thing. Dakota took the salad bowl from the refrigerator. Both hands occupied, she hit the door with her hip to close it.

"No, it'd be an inquisition, right? You have questions."

The invitation to dinner had been to put her at ease. With nothing to lose, he was direct with her. "An inquisition implies that you think I'll grill you, which implies that you're reluctant to give me answers, which in turn implies that you're hiding something."

He made her smile despite herself. Dakota placed the large bowl in the middle of the small, rectangular table where she and Vinny took their meals.

The tiny kitchen was a tight fit for a man who was well over six feet and a woman who measured about five-seven if he was any judge. It made moving around without bumping into one another difficult, if not impossible. After two narrow misses, Rusty decided that maybe it would be best for both of them if he just sat. Brushing up against her was making his thought process fuzzy, sending his mind places it had no business being.

"Let's start with the million-dollar question first— who do you think took your son and why?"

Plunking down silverware on top of light blue paper napkins, she looked directly into his eyes. It was now or never. She either had to trust him, or go it alone.

She made her choice.

"His grandfather, and for a whole host of reasons." Her lips curved. "He's a family kind of guy."

There was no humor in her smile, he noted, and

none in her eyes. Maybe it was an inside joke. And he was standing on the outside. Ordinarily, that wouldn't bother him. But it did this time. More than just a little.

He watched her as she went to get two glasses to set down beside the plates. "What's this family kind of guy's name?"

She paused for a moment, then looked at Rusty over her shoulder. Here came the big payoff. "Vincent Del Greco." She watched his face to see if the name meant anything to him.

Rusty blinked. Vincent Del Greco.

Las Vegas.

The kingpin of organized crime.

Things clicked into place. It was starting to make more sense now. "Then his son is—"

"Was," she corrected. If Vincent hadn't been who he was, she wouldn't be facing this kind of situation. Then again, if he hadn't been who he was, he wouldn't have been dead and they would have been married by now, living somewhere else and enjoying life and their son. "Vincent Del Greco Junior."

Rusty took the can of soda she offered him, opening it mechanically. She'd referred to the boy as Vinny. "That makes your son Vincent the Third."

She took her seat, a smirk on her lips. "We'll add 'counting' to your list of accomplishments."

They would have to get a few things ironed out if he was going to keep working on this case. He might as well get to it. "Who gave you that chip on your shoulder?"

"Life," she retorted. She'd never liked being criticized, even subtly. And the question was a veiled criticism if ever she'd heard one. "And I earned it because I stayed alive."

There was a story there, a story he meant to hear before this case was over. But for now he figured he'd do best to veer back on course. "Why would his grandfather steal Vinny?"

Maybe Andreini wasn't as bright as she thought. "To get him away from me." And maybe he'd been living in a cave these past years and didn't know who and what he was up against. "Vincent Del Greco Senior is not the kind of man who's about to go to family court to plead his case. Nobody tells him what he can or can't do, even if they were brave enough to try. Besides, heads of organized crime syndicates aren't exactly considered model parents. Even Vincent Senior knows that. He'd never win custody the legal way. But he wants my son more than anything in the world."

Her voice had quavered slightly and she bit her lower lip to keep it and herself from breaking. Keeping her eyes on the bowl, she dug the salad tongs into it and commandeered a helping of salad for herself. A helping she couldn't honestly visualize herself eating, not with this new lump in her throat.

She tossed the tongs back into the bowl. They clanged as if signaling the end of a round.

"He wants his grandson, but not his grandson's mother," Rusty guessed.

She raised her eyes to his. And then lifted her chin

pugnaciously. Andreini had hit the nail on the head.
"No, not me."

Given what he had heard about the intertwining
family structure within the Del Greco organization,
Rusty was somewhat surprised. Family seemed to
mean a great deal to the old man. "Why?"

She'd checked her pride at the door when this had
begun. She gave herself no airs now. "Because I'm
only the bimbo that his precious son slept with."
Shaking the salad dressing bottle furiously, she
poured far more on her salad than she would normally
have eaten. Like encroaching orange-and-white lava,
the dressing swallowed up everything in its path. "At
least, that's the way Del Greco sees it."

Rusty picked up the bottle of dressing and noticed
that it was now almost empty. Just as well, he wasn't
a big fan of French anyway. He reached for the salt
instead and sprinkled it on the small serving he'd
taken. "And how do you see it?"

Her hand fisted around the fork she'd just picked
up, Dakota glared at him. "What are you asking
me?"

He didn't rise to the tone she used. Instead he said
mildly, "All right, I'll put it another way. How does
a woman who reads Aristotle wind up with the son
of Vincent Del Greco?"

Dakota forced herself to relax, her grip on her fork
loosening. "So, you picked up on that, did you?" She
was putting him through a lot, she thought. Maybe
she owed him a little background information at that.
What could it hurt? "I was going to college when

Vincent met me.'' That made it sound as if they'd met on campus, she realized. "I met him at the club where I worked putting myself through school. One of the rooms at Caesar's Palace," she specified in case Andreini still didn't get the picture. "Needless to say, it wasn't my mind he was attracted to. At first," she added with a pleased note.

She'd been a showgirl, he thought. He could readily see it. The long legs, the long mane of beautiful hair and the world-weary attitude. It all fit together. But anyone taking the trouble to talk to her for more than a few minutes could see that was where the stereotype ended. She wasn't some bimbo, no matter how Del Greco perceived her.

The salad he toyed with held no interest for him, but the woman he was sitting across from did. More than a little. "Somebody with your brains should have known not to get mixed up with someone like Vincent Del Greco's son."

Hindsight was wonderful. Too bad it didn't work in reverse, she thought. Andreini was right, but three years ago, her life had been filled to bursting with activity. And she'd been flattered by Vincent's attention.

"Someone with my brains was too busy to know who he was, other than some nice guy who kept coming back, night after night, just to see me." She smiled, remembering. Things had been nice then, almost perfect. That should have been her first warning. Life was never perfect. "He sat ringside center. The waiters loved him. He tipped well and didn't throw his weight around. He was kind of sweet, really.''

Rusty saw a smile he hadn't seen before slip over Dakota's lips. A soft smile, prompted by good memories. He found himself mesmerized. ''So he lied to you about who he was.''

Her smile faded around the edges. ''You have a way of cutting to the chase, don't you?'' She sighed. ''Yes, he lied to me.'' It seemed ironic somehow. ''The only person I learned how to trust and he lied.'' By the time she'd found out who he was, she was in love and pregnant. The news, discovered accidentally, almost devastated her. She would have moved out that very day, if he hadn't begged her not to. ''But he told me that he was afraid I wouldn't have had anything to do with him if I'd known who he was, or who his father was, actually. Vincent wasn't about that kind of life. He wanted to get away, break all ties. That was what he told me when he finally broke down and confessed to me who he was. I was angry at first—I had a lot to be angry about. I was pregnant with the grandson of the head of a large crime organization. And I was crazy in love with Vincent.''

Rusty found himself envying a dead man. ''So what happened? Why didn't he marry you?''

Dakota straightened, taking umbrage at the question. She could tell what he was probably thinking, that Vincent just wanted a good time, nothing more. But it wasn't true. They'd meant something to each other.

''He wanted to. I was the one who held out.'' The

truth was that she'd been afraid to marry him. Afraid not just of his connections, but of the marriage failing. She didn't like being confronted with failure. There'd been too much in her life already. "I was trying to make peace with the idea of what I was marrying into. It was Vincent who kept insisting I wouldn't be marrying into anything, that I wasn't getting his family when I said my vows, only him. And that he was serious about breaking all ties. He applied for a job at a private two-year college back east, teaching English, and they accepted him. We were going to get married in Vegas and then fly out to Connecticut to start a whole new life together."

It all sounded like some faraway dream now when she talked about it, she thought. A dream that had been someone else's.

He waited while she paused, knowing not to prod. She would tell him in her own good time and the night stretched out in front of them.

This was hard, she thought. Talking about it was hard. Just as hard now as it had been then.

"I had just finished paying for the wedding dress I'd picked out when I heard the news over the radio. The son of Vincent Del Greco was gunned down outside one of the restaurants his father owned. Del Capo. It's known as a popular mob hangout. I don't know if he was there against his will, or if he'd been lying to me all along." Over the past two years, she'd asked herself that question countless times. There'd been no answer. "All I knew was that I was a widow before I was a wife. A legal wife," she added.

She'd been Vincent's wife in every other sense of the word, supportive and trusting. And loving. But all that was in her past now.

And she had to move forward.

Looking back, she couldn't believe how huge a fool she'd allowed herself to become because she'd fallen blindly in love.

He knew it hurt her to remember, but he needed to have everything as clear as possible. "Did Vincent Senior know about the baby when his son was killed?"

"Oh, he knew all right." He'd found out that Vincent had given her his mother's necklace, the same necklace she'd brought to Rusty, and had hit the ceiling. "When I came home from the shop, the news of Vincent's murder still echoing in my brain, I found two of Del Greco's goons waiting for me. They were there to 'escort' me to the family estate. I went. Not that I had any choice in the matter." She had no illusions that free will was remotely involved. "They would have carried me off in a gunnysack, kicking and screaming if I'd tried to resist."

Rusty had a feeling that she would have put up one hell of a fight before she was taken, he thought. "Then what happened?"

She remembered how afraid she'd been, sitting in the back seat of the stately black limousine, with one of the men beside her, not saying a single word.

"Vincent Senior told me that he had a deal for me that he figured I wouldn't refuse." Her mouth curved at her own deliberate play on words. "He was really surprised when I did."

She'd aroused his curiosity. "What was the deal?"

It wasn't a deal, it was an ultimatum. "That I could stay on the family compound until after the baby was born. That I'd be well paid for my 'trouble.'" She almost choked on the words. "And that after 'it' was over, he expected me to leave quietly, content with the money I'd made with so little effort."

It didn't take a trained ear to hear the way she measured out her words or a trained mind to imagine what she thought of the "deal." "Did you spit in his eye?"

Dakota laughed, some of the tension leaving her. "Nearly. I wanted to. But I had a baby to think about so I just said thank you, but I wanted to think about it if it was all the same to him."

He was surprised that Del Greco had let her get away with that. "And then what?"

"And then I ran." Within three hours after she'd been dropped off on her doorstep, she'd had everything packed and was ready to make her escape. "I had a few friends and they took up a collection for me." She'd made a vow not to touch any of the jewelry that Vincent had given her until it was absolutely necessary. "It got me as far as Laughlin. That was where Vinny was born." The pain of childbirth had been nothing compared to the pain of possibly losing her baby. "In a very pretty little hospital where the nurses are all nuns. It kind of made me feel protected." But the feeling had been short-lived.

There was something almost wistful in her voice. "Why didn't you stay?" At least until she'd gotten her strength back. He judged that she must have been on the run almost immediately.

"Because I'd made the mistake of telling one of my friends where I was going." It had been unavoidable and she didn't blame Erica. Erica had had no choice but to give her up. Dakota would have loved to have just five minutes alone with the man who had hurt her friend because of her. "She'd driven me to the bus station to buy the ticket. Vinny's grandfather had his men 'persuade' Erica to tell them where I was. I found out she wound up in the hospital needing thirty-seven stitches." Dakota's guilt had almost been too much to bear when she'd heard. She'd vowed that as soon as she was able to spare a little money, she'd begin sending it to Erica on a regular basis. She owed her. Big-time. "He made sure she wouldn't be head-lining any more midnight shows on the strip," she added angrily.

Rather than allow herself to dwell on any aspect of the past, she shook off the memory and looked at Rusty.

"So you see the kind of person you're up against. A man willing to do whatever it takes to get his hands on Vinny and keep him." She pressed her lips together to keep the tears back. "I know what he wants. He wants to train my son to take over once he isn't around anymore." Those had been his plans for Vincent. She looked at Rusty. "I can't go to the police with this. They wouldn't exactly be sympathetic about the missing grandson of a crime lord. And even if they did try to get him back, it's not something they'd go about secretively. They'd have to have warrants and make sure to cover their tails every step of the way. That means there'd be different departments in on it. Departments coordinating with each other.'' Andreini knew what that meant as well as she did, Dakota thought. "The more people involved, the greater the chance that someone will tip Del Greco off that the police were out looking for Vinny. There're so many places that man could go in this country, so many places he could stash my baby. If I went to the police, I'd lose any chance of ever seeing my son again.''

She looked down at her food. All she'd succeeded in doing was push it around on her plate. It looked inedible now.

''I don't need an army, Andreini, I need just one soldier. Preferably one who's good at getting in and out of places without being noticed.'' Although she had to admit that the description didn't exactly fit Rusty. He was noticeable, if nothing else. There was something about him, about his bearing even beyond his height, that made you stop and look.

She leaned over the table, her hand resting on his wrist. ''So now you have all of it. Will you help me?'' When he didn't answer immediately, she figured she had her answer. Rallying, she made the best of it.

Always move forward, Dee. Otherwise, you slide backward.

''I'll understand if you say no,'' she told him,

thinking that his silence had already said it for him.
"Vincent Del Greco isn't just some annoying, angry
grandfather. He's very powerful and ruthless, and he
has a long reach."

It took Rusty a second to realize that she was writing him off. "I wasn't thinking about that."

She looked at him, afraid to grasp at hope. "What
were you thinking about?"

"About how you must have felt, standing in that
bridal store, listening to the radio and finding out that
your baby's father was dead."

A small smile rose to her lips. "It was a maternity
shop," she corrected. "I wasn't going to be one of
those vain women who was going to pretend her belly
wasn't out to here while she walked down the aisle."
That had been an incredibly sensitive thing for him
to say. Most men wouldn't have even taken that part
of the story in. "Are you for real?"

Since Dakota wasn't eating her salad, he figured he
didn't have to pretend to eat his. Rusty retired his fork
and pushed back his plate. "What makes you ask
that?"

"No man is that sensitive." And then it came to
her. Her eyes widened just the slightest bit. "Unless,
of course you're—"

"There's no 'unless of course,'" he cut in. "My
sister raised me." There was more to it than that.
"My sister taught me." By example as well as by
word. He figured he could have done a whole lot
worse than to have Megan as his teacher.

His sister sounded like the kind of family she

would have wanted, if she could have put in an order
for one. Instead of losing both her parents when she
was fourteen. ''I think I'd like to meet her sometime.''

''Sure. Why not?'' Maybe meeting Megan might
help her lose that chip on her shoulder. ''Right after
I get Vinny back.''

Dakota rose from the table, the untouched plates of
salad in her hand. ''We,'' she corrected, dumping the
contents of each plate into the garbage. ''After we get
Vinny back.''

Rising, he crossed to the sink where she was standing. He figured he'd start by taking the simplest interpretation of her words, though he had a hunch that
wasn't what she meant. ''Well, sure, he's your
son—''

''No, I mean I'm going to go with you.'' She
dropped each plate into the dishwasher rack and shut
the door. She stood and faced him squarely. ''Wherever this goes, I have to follow it.'' He looked as if
he was going to say something to talk her out of it
and she quickly said, ''I sat home today and thought
I was going to go out of my mind. I can't do that
until you get back. I've got to do something, I've got
to help find him.''

He noticed that she was no longer doubting that he
would find her son. They'd made a great deal of progress over the inedible salads. ''Okay.''

''Okay?'' The easy victory left her surprised and
suspicious. ''You're not going to try to talk me out
of it?''

He looked into her eyes. "Would it do any good?"

"No."

He shrugged good-naturedly, her answer a foregone conclusion as far as he was concerned. Besides, he wouldn't have been able to find it in his heart to tell her she couldn't come with him. "Then I won't waste the effort."

She searched his face, looking for some sign that he was putting her on. She didn't find it. "You know, I think I'm going to like you, Andreini."

Rusty's grin widened. "That'll make things a whole lot easier in the long run. I need to make a few calls, make arrangements and get tickets for us. Tomorrow morning all right with you?"

Since he wasn't giving her any trouble about coming along, she became eager and was honest in her reply. "Now would be better."

He glanced at his watch. It was after six. "I'm not sure we can get a flight out on such short notice."

She caught his arm, hooking hers through it. "Try."

The sudden physical contact was nice. There had to be some flight out tonight, he reasoned. As for the calls he needed to make, there were phones in Vegas, as well.

"All right, John Wayne Airport is just down the road. I'll go upstairs and throw a few things into a suitcase and be back for you in twenty minutes."

Maybe her luck was finally going to change, after all, she thought. Maybe this man who'd come running in response to her scream really was that white knight they wrote stories about.

She smiled at him. "Thank you."

He paused at the door. He wasn't sure what compelled him to break protocol; maybe it was the pain in her eyes that reached out to him. But whatever it was, he felt himself moved and he touched her face.

"Just doing my job," he said softly.

But Andreini wasn't just doing his job, she thought, he was doing more. Much more. He was giving her something to hang on to, something she hadn't really had a few minutes earlier. Relief combined with hope surged through her.

Before she realized what she was doing, Dakota threw her arms around his neck and kissed him.

Chapter 6

Few things actually managed to catch Rusty completely off guard. As a very young boy, because of his brother's abduction, he'd been exposed to the more serious, sadder side of life and, although it had never affected his naturally optimistic outlook, he knew the curves that life could throw without warning, knew that it was best to be prepared for whatever might come his way.

He wasn't prepared for this.

Not the kiss and not the effect it produced, not his reaction to it, although maybe he should have been. It felt as if there was a meteor shower going on within him in reverse, with bright lights shooting off in all directions and traveling heavenward, pulling him upward.

Ingrained reflexes rather than any conscious thought

had him closing his arms around the supple form pressed against him, holding her to him as the kiss demanded deepening.

He willingly obliged.

Damn, this wasn't professional, but it felt like the best thing that had ever happened to him.

With her emotions in complete upheaval, feeling cornered, not knowing who to trust or where to turn, having this larger-than-life gentle hero appear from nowhere, promising to make things right even when she snapped his head off, temporarily unraveled Dakota. Unraveled her, and yet made her whole. She wasn't very good at expressing her gratitude, wasn't good at allowing people to get close to her. She couldn't even bring herself to leave an opening through which they could slip in. But she had to thank him somehow.

Still, her own response to his words had caught her off guard. But it was as if it were somehow preordained that this was the way she was to show him her gratitude. To kiss him rather than say the words.

Somehow, it seemed natural.

Until the kiss took possession of her.

Dakota hadn't expected to do anything other than press her mouth to his. Quickly, neatly, then step back. Nothing more than that.

But she wasn't stepping back. Wasn't moving at all, except perhaps to sway into his tall, lean body. To pull some of the energy from it and cocoon herself in it.

His body felt a great deal harder than it appeared

to be at first glance. The man felt like an entire sheet of muscle from head to toe. Muscle with the power to completely undo her.

She had to be careful, very, very careful.

In a minute.

When she finally pulled back, Dakota wasn't entirely certain there wasn't steam seeping from her ears. The rest of her certainly felt overheated. Overheated in the most arousing, delicious sort of way.

With a jolt, she recognized it for what it was. Desire.

Dakota blinked not once but twice, trying to focus on his face, to pull herself together. Not knowing if she could form coherent words—on her lips or even in her mind. He'd managed to scramble every part of her.

Deceptive, that was the word for it. For him. There was a great deal more going on just below the surface than she had first thought. If she'd spared a single thought about it, her first impression would have labeled Andreini a good kisser, but not a great one. The man knocked the word "great" right off the chart.

Taking a deep breath, she released it slowly before she trusted her voice to not crack and utterly embarrass her. "I bet you're really great undercover."

The wisecrack made no sense to him, but then, his brain felt a little fuzzy around the edges. As did the rest of him. He'd had a few girlfriends and there'd been one a couple of years ago that he'd gotten serious with for a while, but right now it felt as if all the girls he'd ever known before had been only light comic-book fare while Dakota Armstrong was Tolstoy. Multilayered, with substance. And he really wanted substance.

He replayed her remark in his head, striving to not appear like a complete idiot in her eyes. "Because I look younger than I am?" he guessed.

Without thinking, she ran her tongue along her lips. She could taste him there. A shiver raced along her spine and she had to assume military posture to keep from giving herself away.

"Something like that," she murmured.

When was the room going to stop tilting? She was a woman in the middle of crisis, for heaven's sake, why was she reacting this way to a man she didn't know, now of all times? She bit back her annoyance with herself, with him for making her feel this way.

If he didn't get moving, Rusty warned himself, he was going to do something stupid. Such as take her back into his arms and kiss her again and then they'd never get out of here. He had an incredible weakness for strawberry ice cream and she made him think of a delicious strawberry sundae with rich whipped cream piled on top. He knew what happened when he came in contact with strawberry ice cream. One bite would lead to another and then another. It was best not to begin.

Except that he already had.

Squaring his shoulders and his resolve, Rusty moved back and gripped the doorknob before turning around.

There was an odd expression on his face. She told

herself it didn't matter, none of it mattered, but she had to ask. "What are you thinking about?"

"Strawberry ice cream," he said just before he closed the door behind him.

"Strawberry ice cream?" she echoed quietly. What did that mean?

Dakota stared at the closed door for several minutes, shaken by what she'd just done. Shaken by what she'd just felt.

Felt.

It surprised her to feel anything at all. She'd spent most of her adult life numb, inwardly isolated from the rest of the world. By accident at first, by choice later. Her parents' death had left her alone and devastated. Each had been an only child, so there were no aunts or uncles from either side to take her on. Only Social Services, with their practical shoes and their mounds of paperwork. The parade of foster homes and the consequences that eventually came in the wake of her orphaning merely hardened the exterior she'd quickly learned to build up around herself.

Only Vincent had managed to crack that exterior, and look where that had gotten her. Another broken heart. At his funeral, she'd sworn to herself that she would never, *ever* feel anything for anyone again except for the child she was carrying.

It hadn't been a difficult promise to keep. Even if she tried, she couldn't react to anything except with anger. Anger had been both her savior and her cross.

But what was going on inside her right now had

nothing to do with anger. The physical ache that had suddenly sprung up reminded her that she wasn't really meant to live out her life like some Tibetan monk.

"This isn't the time...not the time," she muttered to herself, annoyed that her libido would perversely pick now of all times to spasmodically show signs of life.

She needed to think of Vinny, only of Vinny. Shifting her focus from her son, even slightly, could be a fatal mistake. For all of them. She couldn't afford to make it.

Dakota hurried to her bedroom to pack.

As good as his word, Rusty returned not within twenty minutes, but eighteen. He'd learned to never unpack completely from one trip to the other. His line of work kept him on the road more than twenty-five percent of the time. He didn't mind, as long as he remained successful. It was a good trade-off.

He would have been down sooner, but he'd had to stop to make just one call. To Chad, asking him if he would come by the airport to pick up his car in the morning. Since Chad lived closer to the airport than Megan, it wasn't putting his brother out very much.

Besides, the Mustang was his baby. He really didn't like the idea of leaving it unattended in the lot for the next few days. The airport had a high level of security and an accompanying low level of crime, but a car such as his attracted admirers, not all of whom wanted only to look. Better a little paranoid than sorry was the way he saw it.

Dakota opened the door before his finger had a chance to leave the buzzer. There was a suitcase on the floor beside her. And a stuffed animal under her arm, a droopy-looking teddy bear that had seen far better days.

Rusty didn't bother suppressing the grin that curved to his lips. "You always travel with a teddy bear?"

Rushing to get ready, she'd plucked the teddy bear out of Vinny's crib and tucked it under her arm so she wouldn't forget and leave it behind. Dakota glanced at it now, shifting it so that she held it in one hand.

"It's Vinny's. It's his favorite." Why couldn't she say that without feeling as if her throat was closing up? What was wrong with her? She wasn't a crier, she was a doer. Dakota pressed her lips together, willing her tears back to where they'd been. "I want to have it with me when we find him."

Rusty understood. Leaning over, he gave the bear a closer once-over. The once-champagne fur was now merely a dirty beige. There was more than one set of stitches running through the toy's somewhat lumpy body and if he didn't miss his guess, the bear had seen his share of spin cycles in the washing machine.

"Good idea," he agreed, straightening. "It'll help give your son a sense of security and continuity." Turning, he indicated his car. It was parked directly in front of her apartment. "I'm right out here."

"So you're the one who belongs to that car." It had caught her eye more than once. It wasn't the kind of vehicle that went unnoticed.

He got a kick out of phrasing. "Yup, I'm the one."

Picking up her suitcase, Rusty led the way. She was surprised when he stopped to open the passenger door for her. Politeness and chivalry were far from a given in her world.

"Thanks," she muttered.

Depositing her suitcase next to his in the rear seat, Rusty rounded the trunk and got in on the driver's side. He glanced at her as he put on his seat belt. Hers was still in its original position.

"Buckle up."

Looking down at the teddy bear she was holding and lost in thought, Dakota only half heard him. "What?"

"Your seat belt," he prompted, pointing. "Fasten it. Didn't anyone ever teach you to buckle up?"

She shrugged. "Not exactly high on my list of things to pay attention to." At least as far as she was concerned. There was a child's seat in her car for Vinny and she never went anywhere without making sure he was securely strapped in. Somehow, taking the same precautions for herself hadn't seemed nearly as important.

The car remained idling as he looked at her expectantly. With a sigh, she pushed the metal tongue into the slot. It clicked into place.

"Happy?"

"As a clam," he told her, shifting the car into drive.

Dakota chewed on her lower lip, debating. But she had never been one to hesitate. She'd hadn't had the luxury. She needed to straighten things out between them. Now, before it led to anything else.

"Look, about what happened earlier, I don't want you getting the wrong idea."

A smile played on Andreini's lips. She could see it even though he remained facing forward. "And just what would the wrong idea be?"

Obviously he wasn't going to make this easy. "That I'm willing to take what happened even further—I'm not. That you can do anything you want with me because you're helping me find my son—you can't," she emphasized.

"*I* didn't do anything," he pointed out mildly, pulling out of the complex and melding into the evening flow of traffic. "*You* kissed *me*."

Was he saying that she was trying to instigate something? She'd been governed by momentary, impetuous impulse, nothing more. And he had kissed her back. Enough so that she felt the bottom of her feet growing hot. "I wasn't alone there."

He laughed, turning left at the first major intersection. A sea of headlights converged all around him. People were coming home from work. Or leaving their jobs late.

"If you'd kissed a dead man like that, you wouldn't have been alone." He took the image a little further. "It would have been the first miraculous raising of the dead documented in the last two millennia.'' The light two car lengths ahead of them turned red. He put his foot on the brake and spared her a glance. ''You and I have a business arrangement. You're paying the agency by check, not in trade. I thought that was understood.''

Rusty's tone of voice, leaving no room for misunderstanding, almost made her feel foolish for her uneasiness. ''Yes, well...'' She shrugged, looking away.

The light changed. He stepped on the accelerator again. He was going to put in a call to Savannah first thing in the morning. There were things he needed to know, things about Dakota he couldn't ask outright. Yet. But he did venture one question. ''A lot of people go back on their word with you?''

She didn't like having the conversation turned back around to her this way. Dakota tightened her hold on the teddy bear, trying not to let any of the memories in. ''Enough.''

Whether she realized it or not, there was a great deal of emotion packed into the single word. He looked at her before turning his eyes back to the road. ''I won't.''

It sounded like a promise.

She had nothing else but his word to go on, the word of a relative stranger. Yet something inside her believed him.

Or maybe she just desperately wanted to believe again. In something. In someone.

But caution had been her byword for so long. Old

habits resisted being broken. So all she said in response was, "We'll see," and tried not to hope too much.

Her obvious caution didn't annoy him. It was hard to trust anyone after your son was taken by his grandfather. Not exactly a greeting card scenario. "Yes," he told her quietly, "we will."

They inched their way from one street to another, through the heavy traffic. She reached over and turned on the radio. Christmas carols sliced through the silence. Switching to another station only produced more of the same. She and Vinny were supposed to have gone out today to pick out a tree.

The hollow feeling inside her grew. It wasn't fair. Restless, Dakota turned the radio off.

She glanced toward the profile of the man sitting in the driver's seat. It occurred to her that she hadn't even had his references checked. But who would she have gotten to do that, to investigate the investigator? Besides, time was precious. She'd already let too much go by.

Like it or not, she had to trust him.

The silence was driving her crazy. "How long have you been at this?"

He was wondering when she'd start talking again. "'This'?"

She sighed, impatient again. "Finding kidnapped kids."

It was obvious that she just wanted to be distracted. He could oblige. Talking had never been difficult for him, the way it was for his brother. "Since before I graduated from U.C. Bedford. I started doing legwork for Megan. And then Cade and Sam started asking me to do some canvassing for them, too.''

Because they were departing rather than picking up an arrival, he took the upper ramp as they entered John Wayne Airport. It struck him that the place now looked the way LAX had in its earlier stages. A mind-boggling tangle of lanes all somehow managing to dovetail into one another. There was no stopping progress.

''When they found out that I like tinkering with audio equipment,'' he continued his narrative, leaning out the window to take a parking ticket stub stamped with the time, ''they had me cleaning up ransom tapes that came in, things like that. One thing led to another and Cade hired me when I graduated.''

There had been an unspoken agreement between them that he'd come to work for them as a partner once he had his diploma. Cade treated everyone as an equal partner, not an employee. They all had an equal stake in things.

Rusty grinned, seeing a parking place up ahead. ''If he hadn't, I would probably have hung around, making a pest of myself until he broke down and took me on, anyway.''

She watched as he maneuvered cleanly into a spot that would have given her trouble. ''Why this kind of work?''

He turned off the engine. ''Finding lost kids, bringing them home, helping heal wounds. Can't think of anything else I'd rather do.''

She got out on her side, raising her voice slightly to be heard above the din of departing cars. ''I'd think it'd be depressing, talking to people whose lives have been ripped apart, looking for kids you might not find.''

He retrieved their luggage from the back seat, then shut his door. He clicked the security lock into place before looking at her.

''That's why we don't stop until we find them.''

She fell into step beside him, clutching the bear, aware that he was still carrying her suitcase. ''And you've never failed.''

''Nope.'' Stepping back, he let her go ahead of him.

She turned and looked at him over her shoulder. ''Not once.''

There was nothing hidden in his expression. ''Not once.''

Nothing was perfect. She shook her head. ''I don't believe you.''

He looked at her, lowering his head slightly so that she could hear him without his having to raise his voice. ''I'll be glad to show you the files once we come back. But maybe by then, I won't have to.''

His breath along her neck warmed her and heartened her for some reason she couldn't fathom. She didn't explore the rationale behind it, just savored it for a moment. Relying on pure logic was ripping her to pieces.

Dakota looked around the large terminal. Since it was several days before Christmas, the airport was clogged with pre-holiday travelers and people making trips back home a little early in hopes of beating the last-minute Christmas crowd. It looked as if everyone had had the same idea.

There were a number of different airlines housed within the terminal. Rusty looked up at the overhead schedule of flights, searching for the ones that were departing for Las Vegas.

''Pick an airline,'' he told her.

When she did, they located the flight board and went to the appropriate desk to see if they could book seats on the departing plane. With no luck.

They went through the entire gamut, trying one airline after another. All the flights for that evening were booked.

Frustration ate away at her. ''How can the whole state be flying to Las Vegas on a weekday?'' she demanded after they'd been turned away from their fourth airline. ''There has to be some way we can get a flight.''

Rusty thought a second. ''Maybe there is. C'mon, follow me.''

Before she could ask him what he was up to, he was taking the escalator up to the next level. She hurried after him, confused. The second level housed the gates for arrivals and departures, which wouldn't do them much good without tickets.

''Where are you going?'' she demanded as he walked up the ascending steps.

''To get us a flight,'' was all he said. At the landing, he looked around until he located Gate 23. He

stopped short several yards away, depositing the suitcases. "Wait here," he told her.

Before she could offer a protest, he was hurrying
across to where passengers waiting to board Flight
104 were gathered.

She began to follow him, then decided to stand
back and watch instead. She saw Rusty approach a
couple who looked to be in their early thirties. At first
she thought he knew them, then realized that he was
talking to strangers. Strangers whose expressions
went from curious to sympathetic. She was standing
too far away to hear what Rusty was saying to them,
but whatever it was, it was accompanied with hand
gestures and, finally, an exchange of money for two
slim folders.

As he turned around, he waved the folders at her,
the look on his face nothing short of triumphant.

"What did you do?" she asked as soon as he returned. Behind him, she saw the couple wave at her.

"I got us tickets to Las Vegas." He handed her
one, then picked up the luggage again. "Get ready,
we're about to board."

He was moving a little too fast here. "But how—
The woman at the desk said the flight was all sold
out. And even if it wasn't, there were ten standbys in
front of us."

He nudged her along toward the front of the crowd.
"I know, I just went to the most likely looking couple
and asked to buy their tickets."

She twisted around to look at him. "Just like
that?"

"Well, not just like that," he allowed, lowering his voice so that only she could hear. "We're flying to see your sick grandmother. The doctors aren't sure how much longer she can hold on, but her dying wish was to see you. It being the season of good will, Jill and Harold insisted I take their tickets. They figured they could go on standby and wait for the next flight." The good deed had not come without a price, which had put a huge dent in his wallet, since he'd used cash. "Especially since I paid them twice what each ticket was worth."

She heard only one thing. "You lied to them."

The note of disappointment he detected in her voice bothered him. Still holding the luggage, he turned to look at her. "I did what had to be done to get us on that plane. The sooner we get to Las Vegas, the sooner we can check out if Del Greco has your son."

"There is no if," she said emphatically. "He has my son. I know it." To believe anything else would mean that some unknown person had kidnapped Vinny for who knew what reason. She couldn't go there.

"And Jill and Harold now have an extra two hundred dollars to spend at the tables once they get there," he concluded. "This way, everyone got what they wanted."

"Flight 104 for Las Vegas, now boarding at Gate 23," a disembodied voice announced over the loudspeaker.

"That's us," he said, nodding toward the inner doors being opened. He shifted the luggage, getting a stronger grip. "Now wave to the nice people." Nodding, he indicated the couple that had dropped out of the group. They were standing by the double rows of seats.

Dakota forced a smile to her lips as she passed the other couple.

"You're not as innocent as you look," she whispered to Rusty between lips that barely moved.

Tucking her suitcase under his arm, he showed the attendant at the gate his boarding pass, then looked at Dakota pointedly just before moving down the connecting hall. "I assumed you already figured that out."

She knew he was referring to the kiss and decided it was best if she made no comment on that and just concentrated on the fact that his resourcefulness had gotten them on board.

Their seats were in the middle of the plane. Rusty tucked their luggage away and sat beside her. She looked, he thought, a little paler than she had a few minutes ago. The captain came on over the loudspeaker, telling them they were cleared for takeoff. As the plane began to taxi, Dakota gripped the armrest between them. Her knuckles were white.

"What's the matter?"

It bothered her to admit to a weakness, but anyone with eyes would have seen how uncomfortable she was. "I hate to fly."

To her surprise, he took her hand from the armrest and gripped it in his own. "Here, hang on to me.

We'll be there before your stomach has time to re-connect with the rest of you.''

She said nothing, but he noticed she kept her hand in his. And squeezed hard as they took off. He might not be as innocent as he seemed, he thought, but she wasn't nearly as tough as she tried to pretend.

Since she had long nails and her hand was firmly wrapped around his, he thought it prudent not to mention his observation at the moment.

Chapter 7

They were the first ones off the plane.

His right hand somewhat numb due to the death grip she'd kept on it for the duration of the bumpy flight, Rusty led the way, still carrying their luggage. He shouldered a path for them through the crowd until they reached a small island of space away from the loading gates.

Relieved to be off the plane and on solid ground again, Dakota ran her hand through her hair and took a deep, cleansing breath.

"Now what?" she asked, inclining her head toward him so he could hear her above the continuous din.

He'd been to Las Vegas twice, both times on business, and was only marginally familiar with the airport. "The first thing we do is rent a car and get a couple of rooms for the night."

Rooms meant being stationary. She didn't want to be stationary, she wanted to be moving, to be doing. "But it's only nine o'clock."

"My point exactly." It was too late to do anything now. The main objective for tonight was getting here and they'd accomplished that. A fresh start in the morning was the only way to approach the situation. Besides, Dakota looked tired. "We've got to get organized, come up with a plan."

Someone bumped up against her, pushing her into Rusty. She was quick to recover her ground. "You don't have a plan?" she asked, looking at him incredulously. She had just assumed that he would have everything all arranged.

"Not yet," he told her honestly. Although there was always a master plan in place, working plans came into existence as the action unfolded.

She set her jaw hard. "Well, I do."

Something in Dakota's tone made him uneasy. "And that is?"

She was tired of waiting, tired of games. The only way she knew how to deal with things was head-on. "Confront the bastard."

That was what he was afraid of. "That's not a plan, that's an action, which," he pointed out patiently as he resumed walking, "will get you a very bad reaction." Rusty looked at her as she fell into step beside him. "You're tired, you're stressed out and people in that condition are prone to making some pretty bad judgment calls."

She didn't like being criticized, even if the tone was kind. "Oh, and what do you suggest?"

"A rental car, rooms," he repeated. He saw the skepticism in her eyes. "Let me make a few calls. You don't want to go like the U.S. cavalry into the enemy camp unless you know that the rest of the fighting force is just beyond the ridge to back you up. Deal?"

He waited for her to give him her word. Now that they were here, he had the uneasy feeling that she might do something foolish, such as go off and try to get Vinny back on her own. Del Greco wasn't the kind of man you called out on the carpet.

Stopping again, Rusty set down her suitcase, pinning her with a penetrating look. "I'm not going to have to chain you to your bed, am I?"

"No," she retorted. And then she relented. He was just trying to help. Chewing off his head wasn't going to help them get through this. "It's just that I'm..." Frustrated, she let her voice trail off.

"Yeah." His voice was nothing if not sympathetic. "I know."

Dakota looked at him sharply. "How could you? How could you possibly know what I'm feeling?"

The roller coaster ride she was on had to be tiring for her, he thought. "Empathy is a great equalizer."

Not wanting to get into a discussion with her here, while they were both tired and the possibility of saying things they didn't mean loomed large, Rusty started to pick up her suitcase again.

"I can carry my own suitcase."

''Nobody ever said you couldn't,'' he replied mildly, taking it in his hand. He nodded toward the escalator that was close by. ''I think there's a rental agency on the ground floor just beyond the escalator.''

''There is,'' she murmured, matching him stride for stride, aware that he had shortened his for her sake. Walking normally, he could easily outdistance her.

There were several car rental agencies, neatly coexisting side by side. Their counters were all but obliterated from view by the huddled bodies of disembarked passengers in quest of transportation.

It didn't look as if they were going to get much of a break tonight, Rusty decided. He looked over his shoulder at Dakota.

''Maybe you want to sit down. It looks like it's going to take a while.'' Even the shortest line had eight people in it.

''I'll stand,'' she replied stoically. Holding the teddy bear to her, she stood beside him. When he turned to say something further to her, he realized that she was scanning the crowd.

He looked over the sea of people, mostly incoming, and saw nothing that appeared out of the ordinary. ''What are you looking for?''

''Vinny.'' Out of the corner of her eye, she could see his expression. He was going to say something kind, a charitable remark about her overwrought state of mind. She didn't want pity. Pity only made her angry. ''You never know. Maybe Del Greco's getting ready to fly out of the state. Or even out of the country.'' She set her jaw pugnaciously, ready for an argument from him. Something to sink her teeth into to distract her so she could stop worrying for even a few minutes. ''This would be the airport he'd go to.''

Rather than argue, Rusty nodded in agreement. ''Good point.''

She didn't know whether he was patronizing her or being serious. She didn't ask. All she knew was that it helped keep her sane to be doing something, no matter how far-fetched and hopeless it might seem.

So, while they inched their way up to the car rental counter, she stood and scanned, silently praying that for once a long shot would pay off.

But it didn't.

Forty-five minutes later they finally made their way to the far end of the lot where Bonanza rentals kept their vehicles. She pulled up her collar as the chilly night air swept in from the desert.

When they came to the space where their rental car was waiting, Dakota could only stare. The vehicle was just marginally larger than a Yugo.

''They're kidding, right?'' Very slowly, Dakota moved around the car, eyeing it skeptically. ''Do you think it can even run?''

Rusty fingered the key the clerk had handed him after the paperwork had been completed. ''That's what the man said, although I think that still remains to be seen.'' It wasn't going to be easy, getting into that. Not at his height. "Know the old expression, beggars can't be choosers?"

She frowned, looking up at him over the roof of the lime-colored vehicle. "Yes, they can. They can at least get a car meant for two normal-size adults. This is a Smurf car."

He opened the driver's door and glanced inside. There was no way, he thought. "Smurfs?"

She nodded. "Little blue people." A warm, secure aura temporally surrounded her as she remembered early Saturday mornings when she was six, spent in front of a television set, eating cereal out of a box with her father while they watched the programs. "It was a Saturday morning cartoon—"

"I know who the Smurfs were." He wedged in first her suitcase, then his own into a back seat meant for children. Very small-boned children. "I just didn't think anyone owned up to watching them but me."

The fact that he actually had watched the same cartoons as she had gave them a bond and instantly removed a layer from her armor. "Papa Smurf had a lot of wise philosophies."

Rusty grinned, placing the passenger seat into an upright position again. "For a man who was only six inches tall."

She looked in on the driver's side and shook her head. Any way you looked at it, it was going to be a tight fit. "One thing's for sure, he would have had no trouble reaching the pedals in this car."

"Maybe it's not as bad as it looks." Which he knew was a lie. It was undoubtedly worse. Getting into the driver's seat would be hard, getting out might be impossible. "Besides, what are you complaining about? You're only what, five-six?"

Unconsciously, she rocked forward on her toes. "Seven."

He snorted. That was tiny in comparison. "I'm six-three."

"Really?" She cocked her head as if she were taking full measure. "You look more like six-two to me."

He grinned. "Was that humor?"

Dakota raised a shoulder, then dropped it carelessly again. "Yeah."

"I guess there's hope for you yet," he commented. The wind was picking up. They had to get going, but he really didn't relish stuffing himself in behind the driver's wheel. "A sense of humor is what separates us from all the other animals."

"I thought divorce did that."

The response was so effortless, Rusty had to laugh. "You keep it up and we'll have to see about getting you a comedy gig after this is over."

His smile could be labeled intimate. Warning bells went off in her head. Humor faded from her features. This wasn't going to go any further than was absolutely necessary.

"After this is over, we won't be seeing each other at all," she reminded him tersely.

She'd changed right in front of his eyes. Why? But for now, he thought it best not to ask, not to challenge. "Right. I forgot."

"Well, don't."

He paused, his hand on the rusted section of the door handle. The hell with his resolve. He had to ask. "Is there any reason why your barriers go up as soon as you start being the least bit human?"

She was going to hotly deny his observation, then knew there was no point. So she was honest. And defensive. "Yeah. It keeps me alive."

He looked at her for a long moment. "I'd say it also keeps you lonely."

She didn't need or want to be analyzed. "You can say anything you want," she told him coldly. "As long as you find my son."

"That's the main idea." He started to get in, but stopped with only one leg inside the vehicle. He raised his eyes to hers. "You're pretty familiar with this area, right?"

"I lived here for four years," she replied, her voice guarded. "Why?"

He stepped out of the car again. Being in control didn't necessarily mean that he had to be the one who drove. "Because any way you slice it, this is a sardine can, but there's a little more room on the passenger side than on the driver's side. I thought I'd let you drive if you don't have any objections."

She stood her ground even though he came around to her side. "*Let* me drive?"

She was touchy. He gave her some slack because of what she was going through. Getting into a discussion over word usage was dumb, any way you looked at it.

"Request that you drive," he corrected amiably.

It was hard to pick a fight with a man who smiled so much. "Better." She rounded the hood, crossing to the driver's side. "Okay, get in."

"Easier said than done," he muttered, trying to fold his body into the small space. It took some effort. "If it was any more crammed in here—" he shut the door "—I think my knees would pierce my chest."

She laughed, starting the car. Like a dog shaking off water, it undulated into life. "That's what you get for having bony knees."

He decided it was useless to point out to her that his knees weren't bony, only his position was cramped. "Since we don't have a reservation, maybe you should pick the hotel."

She debated driving to the Desert Rose. Monica and Alan were still working there the last she'd heard and it would be wonderful to actually see familiar faces. But that was exactly the reason she couldn't go there. She was afraid to let anyone know she was here looking for her son.

Not that she thought Monica and Alan, or any of the other people she'd come to know while working here, would give her away willingly, but she'd already learned the hard way that Del Greco's men knew how to extract the information they were after and she didn't want to risk having another one of her friends put through what Erica had suffered. One person on her conscience was more than enough.

So she chose a place where she was sure she wouldn't run into anyone from her past.

''They tell me the Ali Baba is lovely this time of year,'' she quipped, making a right turn at the end of the block.

He gestured as much as he was able. ''Lead on, MacDuff.''

''It's 'lay on,''' she corrected, taking another right. The car in front of them was crawling. Dakota noticed as she turned to check before changing lanes that Rusty was smiling at her. She could use a laugh right about now. ''What?''

She kept surprising him. Maybe that was what he found so attractive. Gorgeous legs, a killer body, hair like ripened sunlight and skin like cream only went so far, after all. ''Aristotle. Shakespeare. Were you going for an English degree?''

He couldn't be further from the truth. Funny, it all felt like a million years ago now. Another lifetime, really.

''Nursing, actually. Considering the kind of life I was exposed to, I thought it might come in handy.''

He wondered if she was referring to organized crime. Just how peripheral had she been? ''That doesn't explain the reading material.''

She smiled. God, but she'd been naive then. Was it only two years ago? ''I was trying to absorb as much knowledge as I could along the way.'' She shrugged, knowing how that must have sounded to him. ''I like knowing things.''

''A nurse, huh?'' She would have to work on her bedside manner, but then, he knew he was seeing her at her worst. Most women weren't contenders for the

congeniality award when their children's lives were
at stake. "Does that mean when we reach the hotel
you can surgically remove this car from my body?"

She laughed. "I can try." Looking at him when
they stopped at the next light, she shook her head.
"You don't give up, do you?"

"No, not in my nature," he acknowledged simply.
"Anything in particular you're referring to?"

She supposed she liked that about him, that he dug
in. She knew what happened to people who didn't.
They lost everything. "Yes. Trying to get me to
lighten up."

And he was succeeding, he congratulated himself.
Marginally. "I figured since we're going to spend the
next few days together, it might not be a bad idea to
get you to relax. Otherwise, you just might snap on
me."

"Maybe at you, but not on you," she told him
pointedly. Did she appear that weak, that vulnerable
to him? "I've been carrying my own weight ever
since I was fourteen."

So that was when the turning point had happened.
When she was fourteen. She'd been robbed of a third
of her childhood. "Maybe it's time you set it down,"
Rusty suggested.

As if she could. "The second I do, someone's going to come by and run me over." She had absolutely
no doubts of that.

"Maybe not."

When you allowed yourself to become too trusting,
the world played you for a fool, and she refused to

be anybody's fool. "Just because I lived and worked in Vegas for four years doesn't mean I'm a betting woman. I like a sure thing."

He wouldn't have thought that of her. She seemed to be a woman who liked living on the cutting edge. Showed that you just never knew. He watched the parade of bright lights go by as she drove. "Read the last page of the mystery book, do you?"

She spared him a look. "Before I decide to buy it, yes."

Other than in situations involving his work, he liked being surprised. "Then why bother to read it if you know how it turns out?"

That was easy enough to explain. "Life doesn't come with a last page to turn to. I take my happy endings where I can."

He studied her profile for a moment. It took him a second to realize that his palms felt itchy. He wanted to reach out and trace the perfect features.

He kept his hands where they were.

"Sometimes you have to risk things to get there," he told her.

"And what have you risked?" she asked, turning the tables. Let *him* answer a few questions for a change. "Been involved with many women?"

"A couple," he admitted vaguely, though he wasn't about to lie to her to make himself out to be something he wasn't. "Between college and work, there hasn't been much time to be involved with my own bed, much less with someone in it."

Just as she thought. A blind man giving a dissertation on the nuances of color. "Well, after you've risked being committed a time or two, come back and we'll talk about that little lecture you were about to launch into, not before."

She certainly got riled easily. "No lecture, just an observation."

"Keep those to yourself, too." Dakota glanced at him and doubted that she'd seen many people who'd looked more uncomfortable than he did. "Unless you don't want any help getting out of that seat."

"I'll be good," he promised, only half kidding.

He rarely felt stiff, except after a particularly grueling workout, but he sure as hell felt stiff now. The trip from the airport couldn't have taken more than twenty minutes, but it felt as if he'd been in that awkward position for hours.

Dakota pulled into a parking lot and they got out of the car slowly. Rusty stood rotating his shoulders and his neck to get his circulation moving again. He could have sworn that everything had frozen and congealed inside him for the duration of the ride. As something clicked into place along his spine, he looked around.

The Ali Baba was a motel rather than a hotel. Clean, at least from outward appearances, but definitely old. Its sixteen units were arranged in a horseshoe pattern framed by an archway that had the words Open Sesame painted over it.

"Cute," he murmured.

She tried to read his expression, wondering if he was being sarcastic. "The sheets are clean and to my knowledge, the board of health has never closed down the kitchen.''

''It has a kitchen?'' he asked, surprised. He maneuvered the two suitcases out one at a time, taking extra care with his. There were things inside he didn't want damaged.

She nodded. ''Small, but adequate. I lived here for a while until I got my own place near Caesar's Palace.'' She saw that he was looking at her with a glint in his eye that she found all too familiar. She'd seen it in the eyes of ringside patrons night after night. ''If you're trying to envision me without clothes on, I hate to disappoint you but we had costumes.''

''I'm sure you did. Caesar's Palace has a first-class reputation.'' He hadn't been envisioning her nude. He found it would be far more tantalizing to envision swatches of material strategically placed along her taut body. But he was only needlessly torturing himself, Rusty thought. She was a client and he'd do well to keep that foremost in his mind.

When she swayed like that in front of him, it was hard to.

Walking up to the manager's office, he held the door open for her and then went in himself. The man behind the counter was dozing. He looked like an aging elf with a faded bushy mustache that appeared to have once been bright red. A fringe of hair, far shorter than his mustache, adorned his bowed head. There was a television set on in the background, showcasing highlights of last week's football games. Huge men repeatedly piled up on top of one another.

Rusty cleared his throat. "Excuse me." The man continued to sleep.

Leaning over, Rusty gently shook him by the shoulder. Near lashless lids popped open to display eyes the color of dirty water.

"What?" the man demanded, scrubbing his hand over his stubbled face. A smoker's cough accompanied the single word for several seconds.

"We'd like two rooms for the night," Rusty told him.

"Ain't got two rooms," the man told them. "Got one. It's the holiday season. Take it or leave it." Blinking, he focused on Dakota for the first time. What passed for a semi-leer sprouted beneath his mustache. "If it were me, I'd take it."

Rusty turned to Dakota. "Want to try someplace else?" Rusty offered, even though the idea of refolding his body again so quickly didn't hold all that much appeal for him.

Dakota debated a second. They were both tired and she didn't feel like being choosy, and something told her she could trust him to behave. He'd had the opportunity in her apartment to push further and to his credit, he hadn't.

"No, we can go someplace else in the morning." She wrote a false name on the ledger, then handed the pen to Rusty. He raised a brow when he glanced at the name but said nothing. He understood her reasons. She looked at the quirky little man behind the counter. "Is the kitchen still open?"

The small eyes darted to the wall clock that was

just behind her. "Nope. But the vending machine works. And there's an all-night restaurant a few blocks down. You can get something there."

He remembered the salads that had been tossed away. Since she'd asked about the kitchen, Rusty assumed that she was finally hungry.

"I'll crawl back into the clown car and get us some late dinner," he offered.

Her stomach pinched in response to the word dinner. "Do you mind?"

"No, it keeps me flexible," he lied. "I'll be back in a few minutes."

Provided he'd be able to get out of the car once he reached his destination, he thought.

First thing in the morning, he promised himself as he left her standing with the luggage, he was going to rent another car.

Chapter 8

After moving the seat as far back as possible, Rusty discovered that getting behind the steering wheel of the compact car wasn't as excruciating an ordeal as he'd anticipated. It definitely wasn't comfortable enough to convince him to not exchange the car for another, larger vehicle first thing in the morning, but for the length of time it took to go to a suitable take-out place and return with dinner, he could put up with it.

Although he wasn't actually familiar with this part of Las Vegas, he'd taken two case-related trips to the city in the past couple of years. Each time he was here, he promised himself that he'd come back when he had some time to just take in the city properly. He hadn't made it yet.

Maybe someday, he mused.

As he drove he studied the area and the way it changed between day and night. The difference was amazing. Bedford wasn't like this. There the change was only a matter of lighting. Las Vegas was a whole different world. It was always ablaze with lights, tourists and activity. In the daytime, however, the city was a brisk, bustling place, full of vitality, of promise that the next spin of the wheel, the next turn of the card, would be *the* one. People were full of hope.

At night, a different atmosphere took hold of the streets. The lights and the tourists were still here, but now the homeless and the hopeless began to appear, creeping forward out of the shadows like silent apparitions, not by ones or twos, but by fives and tens, taking possession of the streets. The sidewalks and doorways now belonged to the homeless and the drifters, to the prostitutes and the runaways—the lost souls who would do anything to get enough money just to make it through to tomorrow.

The latter two groups could be seen staking out various corners, displaying their wares, displaying bodies too quickly used up, faces too soon aged.

Rusty felt a pervasive sadness eating away at him as he automatically checked out each group, ever watchful for runaways, lost sheep who needed to be returned home. Working at the agency had left an indelible mark on him.

ChildFinders concerned itself not only with the missing children their clients paid them to find, but with the ones no one thought to look for. The ones whose faces were stored in a Web site database that had grown woefully too crammed.

Since beginning his association with ChildFinders, Rusty had seen children lost far too often. Arguments and conditions at home became too explosive, too much to endure. Kids ran away to what they thought was freedom only to find themselves truly imprisoned. With nowhere to turn, they took their place amid the streetwalkers, thinking this was just a temporary gig to see them through. A temporary gig that permanently claimed them. All too quickly, their fates were sealed.

Their fates and, eventually, their coffins.

Stopping at a traffic light, Rusty glanced across the street at several women calling out to passing cars. Trying to find takers. There were three of them, three strolling hostesses of the evening, he noted wryly. Two were in their thirties, maybe even their twenties, it was hard for him to tell.

But one was much younger.

Someone honked behind him and he realized that the light had turned green. Rusty stepped on the gas, driving to the next corner and then making a U-turn, temporarily forgetting about the errand that had originally sent him out. He made his way back, driving slower.

She couldn't have been more than sixteen, maybe even less. The layers of makeup she wore made it hard to be accurate.

He could tell by the walk, by the furtive glances over her shoulder while simulating a cocky stance.

She was a runaway. Somewhere, a parent, a sister, an aunt, was wringing her hands, wondering if the girl in the tight leather pants and cheap white faux fur short jacket was dead or alive.

Digging deep into his jacket, not an easy feat by any means, he took out the small digital camera he always kept handy and took several shots in quick succession. He slid the camera under the seat when he got close enough for her to notice him.

Rusty deliberately slowed his car. Like a magnet set on high, the vehicle attracted the streetwalkers, who clustered around it, calling out their offers.

"Looking for some fun, mister?"

"Hey, you don't want either one of them, they're used up. You look like someone who wants something fresh and young." Leaning into the vehicle, the girl who'd caught his attention all but spilled out of her tank top.

"Hey, I saw him first," the prostitute with the ill-fitting silver wig snapped, pushing her competition out of the way.

"The hell you did, grandma. Go find someone your own age."

It was a catfight in the making. Rusty put a stop to it. "I want to talk to her." He nodded at the girl he'd photographed.

The other two withdrew, sullen at being passed over and glaring at the girl. The next moment they were calling to another driver.

Smug, the girl looked at him. "So where do you

want to go to 'talk'?'' Her hand on the door, she
started to open it, but he stopped her.

"Right here," he answered.

Annoyance creased her young face. "You crazy?
I'm not doing nothin' out in the open. Some things
aren't legal anywhere. They'd throw my butt in jail.''

He wondered if she'd been there yet, and what the
experience had done to her if she had. "What's your
name?''

She tossed her hair, trying to look seductive.
"Lisa.''

He could see that she was about to tell him her last
name before she stopped herself. Damn, she was even
younger than he first thought. Close up, she looked
more like fourteen. She should be thinking about her
first prom, not about doing tricks in an alley for mor-
ally depraved men.

"How old are you?''

Her eyes turned into slits as she raised her chin
defiantly. "Old enough to know how.''

And that was the crime of it, he thought. "How
about old enough to have any sense?''

The girl stiffened and started to back away. She
looked around, as if expecting to see squad cars.
"You a cop?''

"No.''

She began to relax a little and took a tentative step
toward his car. "A preacher? Because I've got nothin'
against preachers, but you can't pray over me while
we're doing it.''

A preacher. Megan would have laughed herself

silly if she'd heard that one. And then grabbed the girl by one ear, dunking her head in a sinkful of water until the two inches of makeup dissolved.

"No, I'm not a preacher. Just someone who knows what you're up against."

Bright red lipstick pulled back into a mocking smile that was far too old for the young face beneath it.

"What I'm up against, mister, is your car, but I could be up against you if you just stop talking and let me get in."

Rusty had tracked down a runaway just last month. A girl not much older than the one he was talking to. She'd tried to run away three times on the trip back, but when she and her mother were finally together, the girl had dissolved into tears. Mother and daughter had embraced long and hard. Resolving to make a new start.

Rusty thought about that now, about his vivid recollection of the reunion, as he looked at the streetwalker leaning into his car. "It's almost Christmas. Why don't you call home and talk to them?"

The inviting look disappeared, replaced by anger and contempt.

"Talk to them? Hey, dumb-ass, if I could have talked to them, I wouldn't be here." The desert wind was picking up. She pulled her jacket closer to her, but it did little to protect her from the cold she really felt. "Look, if you're not interested..."

He took out his wallet. "How much?"

At the sight of the wallet, Lisa became all smiles again.

"Now that's more like it." She squinted, trying to make out how much he was carrying. "A hundred."

His hand in the wallet, Rusty looked at her long and hard until she finally flinched.

"All right, all right, twenty-five. But for that you're not getting—"

He didn't want to hear a litany of what she would or wouldn't do for specified amounts of money. It was too degrading for both of them.

"I'm not getting anything," he told her. "But you're getting to a telephone." She looked at him, confused. "I want you to take the twenty-five and call home." He handed her the money.

Her hand closed around the money quickly, pocketing it. "What are you, some guy off his nut?"

"No, some guy who wants to see you off the street and home where you belong."

"Fat chance." She was already backing away from the car.

"You'll never know unless you try," he called after her. "Your family might surprise you."

"Yeah, right."

The girl disappeared around the corner. He had a feeling she wasn't going to call. Rusty stepped on the gas just as the other two prostitutes began to approach his vehicle.

The thermostat in the motel room said the temperature was a warm seventy-eight degrees, but Dakota felt cold as she fought to stave off the icy hand of fear. Pacing, glancing at her watch with a frequency that was making her crazy, she wondered if she was being a fool again. Andreini had seemed as if he was on the level, but had he set her up? By leaving her here alone, was he effectively turning her into a sitting duck?

Was the next person to come in through the door going to have a concealed weapon beneath his jacket?

Twenty-five minutes. Twenty-five damn minutes since he'd left. She could have *cooked* a dinner in that amount of time. Where was he?

Something was wrong.

And she wasn't going to just hang around, waiting to find out what. She'd been too fidgety to unpack anything. Dakota grabbed her suitcase from the floor where she'd left it and hurried to the door.

It opened just as she put her hand on the knob.

Her heart slammed into her rib cage. It took her a second to catch her breath and calm herself. She found herself staring at the side of a carryout paper bag that was already growing translucent. The words China Heaven were embossed in red on the side.

"Room not to your liking?" he speculated mildly as he walked in. Rusty figured it was best not to comment on the wild look in her eyes.

She slammed the door behind him and swung around. "Where the hell have you been? Did they make you kill your own food?"

He made no response to her question, only indicated the bag he set down on the small, wobbly table that barely seated two. "I thought you might like Chinese."

She loved Chinese. That he had gone out of his way to get it took the edge off her concern and made her feel foolish.

Dragging a hand through her hair, she blew out a breath. When she spoke again, her voice was several octaves lower. "Then you were gone all this time because you were looking for a Chinese restaurant?"

He unpacked four cartons, two sets of plastic utensils and the two sets of chopsticks the cashier had thrown in. "Something like that."

He was keeping something back. Dakota studied his face. "Want to be more specific?"

"Why don't you eat?" He nodded at the table as he took off his jacket and tossed it over the back of the chair closest to him. "And while you're at it, work on your trusting skills."

She wasn't about to apologize, although maybe she shouldn't have snapped at him. "I would if I had something to trust."

He looked at her pointedly just before he placed his suitcase on the bed. "Me." With that, he turned his attention to the suitcase he was unlocking.

Curiosity nudged at her and she moved a little closer to peek at what he'd packed for the trip. From what she could see, the suitcase was stuffed with hardware. She looked up at him, puzzled.

"Don't you believe in clothes?"

"Change of underwear, different shirt, different socks." He enumerated what was inside the case by way of clothing. He'd packed them beneath the things he considered essential. "Anything else, I can always buy."

What he couldn't buy was the high-tech equipment he'd carefully placed into the suitcase. He'd brought a notebook computer, a small printer and a few surveillance gadgets that Megan had deemed appropriate and helpful for the kind of work they did. When it came to technology, Megan was never wrong.

"I feel like I've hooked up with Inspector Gadget," Dakota muttered incredulously, watching as he took one thing and then another out and placed it on the bed.

"No 'Go-Go Gadget Copter,' I promise," he murmured, referring to a famous line uttered by the cartoon character, a grin lifting the corners of his mouth.

The familiar reference made her smile. "Is there a gun anywhere in that collection?"

He glanced at her. "I don't believe in guns."

She frowned. She was hooked up with a Boy Scout. "It's not a matter of belief. This isn't Santa Claus we're dealing with."

"If we need a gun, one'll turn up," was all he said.

She didn't care for the vague answer. As she watched, absently eating a serving of chicken lo mein, Rusty hooked up the notebook computer to his cell phone and to the digital camera he produced from his pocket.

Within a couple of minutes, he was e-mailing the photographs he'd taken of the young streetwalker to the office with a note directed to Savannah's attention. He knew she'd long since gone home to Sam and the girls, but she would see his message first thing in the morning when she came in.

> See if you can pull a match from the National Center For Missing and Exploited Children's Web site. Somebody might have reported her missing. She looks familiar. If you find a match, let them know that she was last seen tonight on Eighth and Broadway in Las Vegas. And let me know what you find out. I'll be in touch tomorrow.
> Rusty.

Dakota wasn't good at containing her curiosity. "Who's that?"

He glanced up and saw that she was standing practically at his elbow. The close proximity, sitting the way he was on the bed, stirred him. He directed his thoughts elsewhere. "Savannah?"

"No, the girl in the picture."

She was about to tap the screen, then stopped at the last minute. At first glance, Dakota thought, the girl on the screen might have been her when she was younger and had thought that her looks were her ticket out of loneliness and the dangerous foster home she'd found herself imprisoned in.

But she'd never had to sell herself that way. Still, *there but for the grace of God...*

He pressed the send button and the message disappeared. "Just someone I saw on the way to the restaurant. I think she might be a runaway."

Dakota cocked her head, trying to understand what he was telling her. He hadn't mentioned working on a second case while taking hers on. "No one's paying you to find her?"

He disconnected his cell phone from the telephone jack and placed the phone on the bureau beside the one that came with the room. "No."

"So you're doing this out of the goodness of your heart?" she said sarcastically.

Shutting down his computer, he waited for the screen to go blank. "Yeah."

Dakota put down the chopsticks and looked at him for a moment. The cynical look on her face faded. "The men I know wouldn't."

His gaze met hers. "Maybe you know the wrong kind of men."

Something shifted inside her, something that she knew if she let it, would be her undoing. She was determined to ignore it.

"Maybe," she allowed. She sat on the edge of the bed, covertly watching him. Pretending to be completely engrossed with the contents of her take-out carton. "So, did you have any time while being the Good Samaritan to think about what we're going to do tomorrow morning?"

He'd spent most of his time thinking over their best course of action.

"Yes, I did." She worked those chopsticks pretty well, he observed, wondering who'd taught her. He'd

learned how to maneuver his through the combined
efforts of Tommy Liu and his mother, Amy. He
picked up a set of chopsticks himself and proceeded
to make short work of a serving of sesame chicken.
"We're going to get in contact with Detective Graham Redhawk." Sitting beside her on the bed, he
offered her the contents of his container. "Want to
try some?"

About to decline, she changed her mind. Dakota
deftly popped what amounted to a nugget of chicken
into her mouth. It was good.

The smile on her face as she savored the taste almost made him envious of the piece of chicken.

"Another private investigator?" she finally asked.

Rusty shook his head. He took a little of the white
rice and, tilting yet another container, sprinkled some
onto his sesame chicken. "Police."

The feeling of camaraderie instantly vanished. Dakota rose from the bed. "I told you—"

He stopped her before she could repeat her mantra.
"This is someone we can trust," he assured her.
"We've used him before on other cases. He came
highly recommended. Nothing Gray hates worse than
a kidnapper. And this'll be off the record." She still
looked unconvinced so he explained his reasoning. "I
figure the locals might know Del Greco's comings
and goings enough to help."

Forcing herself to calm down, Dakota resumed eating tentatively. "I'm listening."

"We need to somehow get a bug inside the Del
Greco compound."

That was the word for it, she thought. Compound. A prison. With excellent architecture and beautiful grounds, a prison nonetheless. "Okay. How?"

He held up a hand as he swallowed the helping he'd just taken. "I figure the best way is to just walk right in and plant it myself."

Was he out of his mind? "The best way if you want your wife to collect on your insurance policy." She snorted, clearly disappointed even as her sweeping glance criticized him. "I thought you were smart."

"I am," he said unselfconsciously. "And I don't have a wife." The correction was left-handed. "We find out where Del Greco gets his groceries from, I can buy off the delivery truck driver, make the delivery myself." She still looked skeptical. But it was simple. The best plans usually were. "Man's got to eat, right?"

Reluctantly she nodded. He had a point and it might work. But she was uneasy about his calling the police in the first place. "But why do you need this Redhawk guy?"

That explanation was even simpler. "Why spin wheels needlessly? The police probably have that kind of information on Del Greco on file."

That sounded pretty far-fetched to her. "His grocery store?"

Obviously she didn't have a healthy dose of paranoia. "You'd be surprised what kind of information they gather in hopes of finding something to pin on him that won't slide off. Don't forget, they got Al

Capone on income tax evasion, not bootlegging or any of the countless murders he was responsible for.''

Maybe it was time to start trusting him, she thought. After all, so far he'd given her no reason to not trust him. ''I've got something they can pin on him.''

He stopped eating. Had she been privy to some crime organization execution and was willing to testify now to put her baby's grandfather away? ''What?''

She pressed her lips together, watching his face. ''I have a diary.''

None of the main members in the Del Greco organization struck him as the type to put pen to paper. ''Yours?''

She shook her head. ''Vincent's.'' She could see Andreini was taken aback by the information. ''He made it a point to stay on top of what has happening. The trade deals, the protections and eliminations. Said it was his insurance policy to get out.'' Losing her appetite, she put down her carton and retired her chopsticks. ''Except he never got to use it. He was gunned down by a rival gang before he had the chance.''

''And you have the diary?''

She nodded. ''He gave it to me for safekeeping.''

''Where?''

Rising, she crossed to where her large purse lay on the floor. Pulling out a thick, black-covered book, she tossed it onto the bed. Heavily marked blue pages rustled as they landed.

"Here."

Food forgotten, Rusty stared at the tome. "Why didn't you say something earlier?"

The shrug was vague, evasive. "I wasn't sure if you were on their side or mine."

Had they made that much progress in the last few hours? Hours, hell, in the last few minutes? "And now you are?"

"Enough to show you the diary." She opened another carton and saw that he had bought egg rolls, too. "I thought if worse came to worst, I could trade it for Vinny."

"If they knew you had this, your life would be in serious jeopardy."

He'd surprised her. Anyone else would have leaped on the possibilities that possession of the diary opened. He saw that if Del Greco knew she had this, she wouldn't live to see another day.

Dakota barely nodded. "Yes, I know."

Picking up the diary, Rusty began to thumb through it. From what he saw, the handwriting inside was surprisingly neat. It was as though Vincent had been preparing to have it read by someone.

He glanced at Dakota. "Looks like I'm going to be doing a lot of reading tonight."

Chapter 9

Dakota approached the large queen-size bed that suddenly seemed to dominate the room and paused. Slowly she turned toward Rusty, wariness and defiance in her every movement, her every syllable.

"You don't mind taking the couch?" Quietly holding her breath, she waited for him to renege on the agreement about the boundaries of their relationship.

Rusty raised one shoulder in a careless shrug. "Couch, floor, it's all the same to me. I can sleep anywhere if need be. I've been known to sleep hanging on a hook in a closet." He was describing his brother-in-law's ability, not his own, to put her at ease. But he didn't see a smile on her face in response, just the same wary look. "That's a joke."

She was trying to decide whether or not she believed his disclaimer. Whether or not she'd find him beside her in the middle of the night, a different man once he was concealed by the cloak of darkness. Still, she brazened it out. "I had a feeling."

She was nervous, he thought. He could see it in her eyes, if not in her expression. Was she actually afraid of him? "You didn't smile."

Crossing back to the table with its empty containers, crumpled napkins and discarded chopsticks, her expression remained impassive. "I'll smile after we get my son back."

Maybe she wasn't afraid, maybe it was just unhappiness he saw in her eyes. "Then I guess I've got some reading to do."

Dakota gathered up everything from the table and tossed it into the small, colorless wastepaper basket in the corner. It barely fit. Rusty was already making himself comfortable against a corner of the sofa. She nodded at the book in his hand. It had been a permanent part of her purse for the past two years.

"You think reading that'll help?"

There was a lot here, he mused, flipping pages. Vincent obviously didn't believe in being terse. Rusty glanced up at her. "It couldn't hurt."

He began to read in earnest, trying to not think about the woman who was lying not ten feet away from him.

Rusty had no recollection of dozing off, but he must have. The sound of weeping nudged its way into his consciousness, mixing with half-formed dreams of missing children and baby-faced prostitutes. Backlit by the panorama of lights, he saw Lisa walking toward him. She was sobbing pitifully, her body bruised and battered, her arms outstretched to him in supplication.

With each step she took, her face changed a little, reforming by degrees until by the time she reached him, she was no longer the girl he'd tried to help tonight, but the woman.

Dakota. Dakota was crying. Pleading.

His eyes flew open, the gritty residue of sleep clinging to his lids. The pain in his neck registered somewhere on the perimeter of his consciousness as he searched for the actual source of the sound.

It hadn't been a dream. It *was* Dakota. She was asleep on the bed, the comforter gathered around her, her body bunched into an almost fetal position. And she was crying.

"No. Get away from me. Please. No. Don't. Please, Jamie, don't. No!"

The agony and terror in her voice tore his heart. Rusty was on his feet immediately, the diary falling from his lap to the floor. He almost stepped on it, hurrying to her.

"Dakota, wake up, you're having a nightmare." The words didn't seem to penetrate the heavy drape of sleep surrounding her. Placing his hand on her shoulder, he shook it gently. "Dakota."

She shrieked then, twisting and turning away from his touch. Bolting upright, she shrank back against the headboard as if she were trying to climb away.

Her eyes were wide, unseeing and panicky. The sound of her heavy, shaky breathing filled the room.

"Dakota, it's me, Rusty. Wake up. It was just a bad dream."

Without thinking, wanting only to make her feel protected, secure, Rusty put his arms around her and pulled her to him, trying to comfort her any way he could.

Enraged, still held fast by her dream, she began to beat on him. "Get away from me, Jamie, get away."

Rather than pull away, Rusty caught hold of her hands and held them in his. Who the hell was this Jamie and what had he done to her?

"Dakota, it's me, Rusty. Rusty, not Jamie. Nobody's going to hurt you, do you understand?" he said firmly, then his voice softened. "I promise. Nobody's going to hurt you," he said as he released her.

Reality began to seep in as the clouds of sleep faded from her brain. Her eyes focused on his face. On her surroundings. Shaking, Dakota gulped in air, struggling to pull herself together.

It had been so real. Too real. Ten years had melted away tonight as the past and its buried horrors claimed her. It had been a long time since she'd had that nightmare. She felt as if everything was falling apart around her.

"Right," she finally managed to get out. "A bad dream."

But even as she said it, he knew it wasn't true. It wasn't just a bad dream. This nightmare had its roots in the past.

"Want me to sit here and talk to you until you fall asleep again?" he asked gently.

The offer coaxed a half smile from her. "Why? Are you planning on boring me to sleep?"

"It's been known to work." He looked at her more closely, resisting the temptation to put his arms around her again. "You're shaking like a leaf."

She was and she hated the way it made her seem. Weak. Vulnerable. Dakota wrapped her arms around herself. "Not very original, Andreini."

He wondered what it would take to get her to call him by his first name. "But accurate." He looked at her. "Want to talk about it?"

"No."

She said it so emphatically that she confirmed his suspicions that it had been more than just a dream. She'd been reliving something. It didn't take a genius to know she'd felt powerless against what was happening.

Maybe Jamie had been some kind of a nickname she'd used for Vinny's father. "Were you dreaming about Vincent?"

"Vincent?" The question was so ludicrous, she stared at him, trying to comprehend how he'd gotten that idea. "No." It was a trick to get her to open up, she realized. To spill her guts. Fat chance. "I said I don't want to talk about it."

Though he gave the impression of being mild mannered, Rusty was not the type to back away easily. "Sometimes leaving things bottled up makes them worse. Like when you shake a can of soda. When you finally open it, it winds up exploding all over the place.''

Did he think she was going to come unglued at the wrong moment? He didn't know her very well. ''Afraid of an explosion?''

She was making a habit out of turning things around. ''Just thinking of you.''

She sniffed. Yeah, right. As if anyone had ever thought of her. Not even Vincent. If he had, he wouldn't have lied to her about who he was. He wouldn't have been at that restaurant the day he'd been killed.

''Well, think of Vinny and how we get him back,'' she retorted. She thought of what he'd said about his plan. ''Or are you still making it up as you go along?''

''Fifty-fifty.'' He'd given it a lot more thought after she'd fallen asleep. ''After I plant the bug, we listen for Vinny or for any mention of where Del Greco's keeping him.''

The urge to burst right into the crime lord's house to search for her son was still with her. But Rusty was right. If Del Greco was keeping Vinny somewhere else, it would be pointless to enter the compound like that. Pointless and stupid.

Reluctantly, she gave it her approval. ''Sounds like a plan.''

Unwilling to be sidetracked, Rusty studied her for a long moment. ''Was it one of the foster fathers?''

Anger flared within her. ''Mind your own business.''

His eyes never wavered from her face. "Right now, you and everything about the case is my business."

She glared at him. Slowly, the anger died away. What was the point of lying anymore? With a shrug, she shook her head.

"Brother," she corrected. "Foster brother. Jamie." She repeated his name with all the venom that vermin like him deserved.

He wanted to hold her, to tell her it was all right. That whatever had happened to her in the past wasn't her fault. "Did he—"

Her head jerked up, her eyes forbidding him to form the words. "What do you think?"

He felt a sudden rage inside, a rage against predators that preyed on helpless children to satisfy their own twisted needs. But he knew that what she needed now was calm. "Did you tell anyone?"

"Yes, I told someone." Exasperation fueled the anger in her voice. "For all the good it did."

He sat beside her on the bed, his voice gentle, soothing. "What happened?"

She wasn't going to cry about that. Not after all this time. Damn Andreini for making her feel like crying. She struggled to divorce herself from the memory and from all the nights she'd lain in terror, waiting for him to come into her room again, a pipe she'd found at a construction site hidden under her pillow.

"He was theirs, I wasn't. They didn't believe me." The sigh that escaped was shaky. "He was so beautiful when I came to live with them. Tall and blond and he had this really nice smile. I was so flattered when he started paying attention to me." She pressed her lips together. She'd been so stupid, she thought. "Until he began paying too much attention."

"What did you do when they didn't believe you?"

What could she do? "I ran away. Except I wasn't very good at it." Her smile was rueful. "Social Services found me and brought me back. The situation got worse." She touched no details, not even in her own mind. "So I ran away again." She laughed shortly. "They found me again. Eventually, I got better at running away until one day, they didn't find me. I've been on my own ever since." At least she could sleep nights without worrying about someone coming in.

Bile rose in Rusty's throat. Jamie had raped her. Raped an innocent girl that tragedy had brought into his home. Wherever he was, he deserved to be drawn and quartered and then left to rot in hell. Anyone could see, despite her flippant remarks and behavior, that Jamie had left his mark on her.

"It wasn't your fault," he told her gently.

The effects of the nightmare lingered, reminding her of how awful she'd felt. How tainted. "It happened anyway."

He took her hands in his. This time, she didn't resist. "But it wasn't your fault, Dakota. And things happen. Good, bad, they happen and we have no control over them."

Ashamed of her lapse, she rallied. "Like kidnappings?" she asked cynically.

He looked at her significantly. "Like falling for someone."

Feeling almost embarrassed, she withdrew her hands from his. "You always try to put a positive spin on everything?"

He was guilty as charged and not ashamed of it. "Better than not."

"I suppose." She dragged her hand through her hair and caught her reflection in the window. The world outside was swaddled in darkness. "God, I look like hell."

"Not hell," he contradicted, smiling. "Purgatory, maybe."

She looked at him blankly for a second, then understood. "Oh, right. The halfway house between heaven and hell. I'm not sure whether I should be flattered or insulted."

"Positive, always pick the positive, remember?" He began to rise, then stopped. "My offer still stands. I can sit on the bed until you fall asleep again."

She felt silly for the scene she had caused. Except that it had seemed so real to her, so haunting. "Keeping watch over the crazy woman?"

He countered her sarcasm with a fragment from his past. "My mother used to have nightmares."

She kept forgetting that they had that in common. Because he seemed so well adjusted, it was hard picturing Rusty with any turmoil in his life. "Was that because of your brother's kidnapping?"

He nodded. It had gone on for years, even after Chad had returned. When Mary Andreini wasn't staying in a sanitarium. "I used to stay with her until she fell asleep."

"How old were you?"

He shrugged, not remembering exactly. "Six, maybe seven."

She shook her head, a quiet laugh escaping her lips. The funny thing was, she could actually visualize him doing that. Sitting and holding his mother's hands the way he'd tried to hold hers. Solemn-eyed. "Quite a switch, the little kid sitting up with his mother to make her feel safe."

He'd never thought about it much one way or another. It was just something he'd done. His mother had been in despair and he'd wanted to make her feel all right again. It was years before he'd understood that he never could. That his mother had slipped away into a world where ex-husbands didn't kidnap sons and where things were safe and happy.

He shrugged. "You do what you can when you love someone."

She waved him away. "I'll be okay. You don't have to stay and guard me." Dakota slid back down on the bed, moving her arm under the pillow and bringing it closer to her. She heard him cross back to the sofa. "You can go on reading if you want," she told him.

He smiled to himself, knowing what she was saying. It was the only way she could save face and still have him stand guard, so to speak. "Thanks, I think I'll do that. As long as you don't mind."

Raising her head, she looked over her shoulder at him. The man knew.

That he wasn't rubbing her face in it or making a joke at her expense was more than a point in his favor.

Without a word in response, she curled up and closed her eyes.

This time she slept more peacefully.

She woke up to the sound of his voice. It wasn't entirely an unpleasant sensation, although she fought with disorientation for a moment.

He was on the telephone, making arrangements with someone.

It took her a second to realize that there was more than a glimmer of daylight pouring into the room. How long had she slept?

He replaced the receiver in its cradle just as she sat up.

"What time is it?" she demanded. There was a sour taste in her mouth that went with the heavy feeling in her heart. Vinny was still gone. Was she ever going to get him back?

He'd checked his watch just before making the second call. "Almost eight."

"Almost eight?" she echoed.

She never slept that late. Vinny was always up by seven, if not before. Her lack of sleep the night Vinny was kidnapped had caught up with her. She stumbled to her feet, abandoning the comforter she only vaguely realized he'd thrown over her.

He'd shaven, she noticed. The faint stubble that had been coming in last night was gone. The unshaven look had made him seem a little more manly, more in control. "Shouldn't we be—"

"We are," he replied, anticipating her question. "I've made arrangements to get a van so we don't get crammed during surveillance and I've just talked to Detective Redhawk about getting information on Del Greco's marketing habits."

He'd been busy. She still didn't like the idea of the police—any police—being involved, but she bit back her protest. Andreini seemed to know what he was doing. "This policeman of yours, he's on the night shift?"

He'd gotten the number from Chad before leaving last night. His brother was friendly with the man and his wife. "I called him at his house." He picked up on her wording. "And Graham Redhawk doesn't belong to anyone, except for maybe his family and that god-awful pink Cadillac he's had forever."

She thought of the '64 blue-and-white Mustang in which he'd driven them to the airport. There'd been genuine affection in Andreini's eyes when he'd looked at the vehicle. "People in glass houses shouldn't throw rocks."

He arched a brow. "If you're referring to my Mustang, it's a classic."

Dakota laughed. "I'm sure Detective Red Dog—"

"Redhawk," he corrected.

The name had slipped her mind. "Redhawk," she said, "thinks the same thing about his 'god-awful pink Cadillac.'" She shifted her focus, growing serious again. "More importantly, do you think he'll help?"

"He already said he would." He liked the way the smile, tinged with relief, slipped over her lips. "Gray's a straight arrow—no pun intended—but he figures there comes a time when you have to bend a few rules to catch the bad guys, and in his opinion there are no criminals worse than kidnappers."

She ran her hand through her hair, trying to fluff it up. It felt plastered to her head. And somehow, it mattered that she didn't look like walking death when he looked at her. "And in your opinion?"

There was no hesitation. "I agree with Gray." And then he looked at her, remembering the anguish in her sobs. "Except that maybe I'd put guys who force themselves on little girls first."

She flushed. There was nothing she hated more than pity. "Look, about what happened last night—I don't want you feeling sorry for me."

He spread his hands in a show of mystification. "Never occurred to me. I always thought that feeling sorry was a waste of positive energy."

She wasn't sure he was telling her the truth, but she appreciated the effort. "As long as we understand each other."

He had a ways to go before that happened, he thought, but he was trying.

He also needed, he thought, to get out of this small, confining space because having her so close was punching small holes in his resolve. And a man had only so much of that to go around.

"Want to get some breakfast?"

She looked at the telephone on the scarred coffee table beside the sofa. "Shouldn't you be here in case he calls back with results?"

Rusty patted his pocket. "I gave him my cell phone number. Besides, it should take him at least a couple of hours to wade through the reading material before he comes across something as insignificant as what supermarket Del Greco trusts to get his order right."

There was a vague movement in the pit of her stomach that she took to indicate hunger. Yes, she wanted breakfast. She wanted other things, as well. The fact that she could even acknowledge the growing attraction she felt toward Andreini made her feel like a terrible mother.

A terrible mother who needed a shower. She looked toward the bathroom uncertainly.

He read her thoughts easily enough. "Why don't you take a shower first?" he suggested. He saw the wary light come into her eyes. She'd slept in her clothes last night, no doubt as a precaution. "The bathroom door's got a lock on it."

That didn't make her feel any more secure. "Locks can be picked."

"And doors can be broken down," he pointed out. "But it's not going to happen." He looked her squarely in the eyes. "You're really going to have to trust me at some point, Dakota."

Her attraction not withstanding, she wasn't a fool.

Dakota held up an index finger. "Up to a point," she clarified.

His gaze never wavered. "This might be a good place to start."

She *could* use a shower. "All right. But I know Akido." She cited a new form of martial arts she was only vaguely aware of. What she did know was how to deliver a paralyzing blow to where it really hurt, but she figured that the martial arts reference sounded far more in control.

"I'd like a demonstration sometime," he told her mildly, then added with a grin, "From a safe distance away, of course."

Having little choice if she wanted to get clean, Dakota decided to trust him for the duration of the shower. But she still locked the door. Just in case.

He glanced at his watch when she walked out of the bathroom.

"That had to be the fastest shower on record," he remarked. "You couldn't have been in there more than five minutes."

"Seven," she corrected, strapping on her watch. She'd timed herself. "I only linger in a shower if there's a reason to."

He had the distinct impression there was more to the sentence than she was saying. As in, she only lingered if there was someone to linger with.

He shook his head. What was the matter with him? Not even nine in the morning and he was making himself crazy with thoughts he had no business having.

He wasn't sure just what was going on in his own head because for him, keeping the line between business and pleasure had never been a problem before.

But he had to admit that he'd never worked a case where the victim's mother was attractive enough to melt butter at twenty paces.

Closing the notebook he'd been writing in, he rose to his feet. "Okay, let's go get some breakfast."

Dakota still had her doubts. She looked at the dormant telephone. "You're sure this detective can reach you?"

He slipped the notebook into his breast pocket. "As long as the signal comes through. And if it doesn't, the cell phone has an answering machine built into it."

Dakota was fresh out of objections and hungry. "Okay."

When she was next to him, he realized that her hair was still damp. "Don't you want to dry your hair first?"

She touched the ends as if she'd forgotten about that. The light streaming into the room was abundant and warm. She shrugged. "The sun'll do that."

He'd never met anyone so careless about the way she looked. And who looked so damn good at the same time.

Forcing himself to reroute his thoughts, Rusty opened the door for her and waited until she stepped outside.

Chapter 10

The restaurant they went to for breakfast wasn't too far from where he had seen Lisa. He knew that there was no reason for her to be there at this time, but he looked anyway, hoping that she wouldn't stray too far until someone came for her.

Provided someone came.

Their identical orders of ham and eggs, given to the waitress whose hair was just a shade too bright to be called auburn, arrived quickly. Rusty made short work of his.

Dakota, he noted, seemed intent on rearranging hers on the plate after each small bite. As a result, he was finished eating while she appeared not even to have started. How did this woman ever keep up her strength?

Studying her as he sipped his coffee, Rusty shook his head. "You eat like a bird."

She smiled at that, raising her eyes to meet his. "No, I don't." With effort, she swallowed another bite. But everything that hit her stomach felt like lead. And would probably continue that way until she had Vinny back. She'd resigned herself to that. Even last night's late dinner hadn't gone down well. "Birds usually eat up to twice their body weight in a day. Takes a lot of energy to fly around like that," she added.

He grinned, raising his near-empty cup in a mock toast. "I stand corrected. What did you do—" he wanted to know "—swallow an encyclopedia?"

"No, I just liked to read a lot." She toyed with her fork, trying to sublimate the restlessness that insisted on rising to the surface no matter what she did. "Reading took me away from where I was."

Everyone needed a form of escape. "How long were you in the system?"

She began to tell him that it was none of his business, but decided not to. He'd only find another way to ask the question later. "Three years. I decided to stick it out long enough to graduate from high school and then I took off. That time, nobody came to look for me. Or if they did, they didn't find me."

"Maybe they didn't look because you were eighteen." An eighteen-year-old seemed far too young to be considered a legal adult, he mused. Most eighteen-year-olds had very little sense of reality and responsibility unless they'd been forced to grow up too fast.

It occurred to him that, because of circumstances, both Dakota and he had. And that it gave them something in common.

She shook her head. "Seventeen. I skipped a grade in elementary school."

Elementary school. Even as she said it, it seemed as though that had been a completely different world. She'd had a mother and a father back then, as well as a baby sister. The word family had meant something to her, instead of just being six letters surrounding an empty feeling.

He tried to envision what she'd been like then. Bright, studious. Hopeful. If he looked really hard, he could almost detect a trace of that in the woman who sat in front of him. But then, the next moment, it was gone.

"How does a potential prodigy wind up as a Las Vegas showgirl?"

The laugh was short, dismissive. She'd wound up better than most runaways. But that was because she'd never been down on herself, only on those around her. The ones who tried to strip her spirit away.

"Even potential prodigies have to eat. I lied about my age, said I had experience and studied what the other girls did on stage." A flicker of a smile graced her lips. "I'm a quick study. It's not a bad life if you don't let it get to you. Besides—" she turned to her coffee, taking a sip and making a face before setting the cup down "—I had plans."

"Which were?" His voice was low, coaxing, just interested enough. Or so he thought.

Dakota looked up at him sharply, suddenly realizing she was sharing far more than she'd intended or wanted to.

"What is this, a segment for *Biography*?" She'd never trusted too many questions. He was digging for something. What? "Why all the questions?"

In the face of her suspicions, he shrugged innocently. "Just trying to get to know you."

"Why?" She wasn't buying his excuse. There had to be an ulterior motive. Sarcasm dripped from her voice. "Will it help us get Vinny back?"

He shrugged carelessly, finishing his coffee. "You never know." His eyes met hers again. They were beautiful, he thought, but so filled with pain. He caught himself wanting to alleviate it. Not just by finding her son, but by making up for what the world had tried to do to her. He'd never come across a plea for help, silent or otherwise, that he could turn down. "Besides, I'm curious."

Her eyes went flat. She turned her head, looking out the window without seeing the street just beyond. "Don't be."

If he were in the habit of giving up that easily, he would have changed his line of work. "You know, my brother was kind of like you. Not as snippy, but just as closed-mouthed."

Her head snapped around. "Snippy? I'm snippy?"

He knew that would get her going, but hid his smile. "Bad choice of words, probably. My vocabulary isn't the most accurate." Rusty paused. "Just my instincts."

"Oh, and what do your instincts say?" she asked sarcastically.

"That you could use a friend." He reached for her hand, placing his over it.

She jerked her hand back, but there was a small, reluctant feeling in the center of her indignation that she tried to squelch. She couldn't let herself fall into that trap, the trap of leaning on someone, no matter how fleetingly. She'd already seen where that led.

"What I could use is an investigator."

"That, too," he allowed. "But you're paying for that."

She eyed him for a long moment. "And the friend comes free?"

"Yes."

"Wrong," she contradicted coldly. "Dead wrong. Nothing comes free. One of the first lessons I learned."

The lessons belonged to a past she didn't want to reexamine, except as far as it helped keep her determined to never again allow herself to be in a position where she could be taken advantage of. Where she could be hurt in countless ways.

She pushed her plate away with finality. "And a lesson you should learn is that if you're determined to save souls, you're in the wrong business. Get yourself some sackcloth and ashes and find a shelter full of people to minister to. I don't need saving, or whatever it is you think you're doing."

''Just talking.'' He put his hand over the mouth of his cup as the waitress approached, ready to pour more coffee. He smiled at the woman. ''I'm fine, thanks.''

''You sure are, honey,'' the woman said, giving him a look that could only have one interpretation. ''You sure are.'' Winking at him, she glanced at Dakota's cup, saw that it was still full and sauntered away.

''Why don't you go and save her soul?'' Dakota prompted. ''Or take whatever she's got to offer. She looks like she can talk. For a while, anyway.'' The woman would probably be all over him in a heartbeat, Dakota thought. And she supposed that the waitress couldn't be faulted for her taste. The man was very attractive.

Rusty wasn't about to let himself be sidetracked by the switch in focus. He saw through it. And, in his own way, he felt he was making some progress. She'd opened up a little.

''You throw up a lot of roadblocks, Dakota, but I think I'm getting past them anyway.''

''Think again,'' she said defiantly. There was no way he was getting anything else out of her that didn't directly have to do with Vinny. She wasn't paying him good money to play twenty questions about her personal life. ''So what are we going to do, spar over bad coffee, or get moving?''

The liquid under debate was fair to middling. He'd had better, but he'd certainly had worse. Rusty kept his voice low, thinking it best not to give offense to whoever was responsible for it.

"You think this is bad coffee, you should try my sister's. Coffee so thick, you could break a shoulder diving into it."

She shook her head at the image. "You dive into coffee a lot?"

He grinned in response. "Keeps me moving." He peeled off a twenty and left it on the table. "Okay, let's go."

She looked at the bill. "Breakfast wasn't nearly that much, don't you want your change?"

He left the twenty where it was. His hand to her elbow, he guided her to the door. "The waitress looks like she can use it."

Dakota pushed the door open with the flat of her hand. "Right, to fine-hone her skills."

Habit had him glancing up and down the street before crossing to where the car was parked. "No, for her little girl."

She stopped, looking at him curiously. The waitress hadn't acted as if she recognized him. "You've been here before?"

"No." He opened her door before moving to the passenger side. "She's got a picture of a little girl in a wheelchair taped to the side of the cash register."

She hadn't even seen that. Getting behind the wheel, she glanced at him with grudging admiration. "You don't miss much, do you?"

"No, not much," he affirmed. He reached for the seat belt, then decided there was no need. In the event that they were in an accident, he'd be wedged in the car anyway.

The cell phone rang just as she was about to start the car. Immediately alert, she dropped her hand from the ignition key.

"Answer it."

Rusty was twisting around as best he could. "I'm trying, I'm trying."

But the cell phone was in his back pocket and sitting the way he was, it was impossible to retrieve. Watching his futile effort for a second, Dakota muttered under her breath and reached around his waist to dig into his rear pocket.

The sensation of her body pressed against his, her hand digging almost intimately against his posterior was definitely not an unpleasant one and he found himself smiling down into her face as she struggled to pull the cell phone out.

Her flashing eyes only heightened the feeling for him.

"Here!" she declared, slapping the cell phone into his hand and straightening. She could feel her heart racing and refused to believe it had any other stimulus than the ringing phone.

The slight smile on his face made her feel that he was reading her mind. Dakota flushed as she watched him flip open the phone.

"Hello?"

"Rusty?" The voice on the other end was deep, resonant. "This is Gray, where can I meet you?"

As Dakota strained vainly to hear both sides of the

conversation, Rusty gave the police detective the address of the rental agency that was to be their next stop. It wasn't far from where they were.

"I can make it in half an hour," Gray told him.

"We'll be there," Rusty promised. The other end of the line went dead and Rusty flipped the phone closed.

"Well?" she demanded, wondering if the other man had said something significant.

"Sounds like we're moving forward." He looked down at the phone in his hand. The thought of trying to get it back into his pocket was daunting. "Maybe I'd better just leave it out."

"Good idea." Her response was terse.

Pink color crept up her cheeks in direct contradiction to her tone. Rusty found himself being fascinated.

Detective Graham Redhawk looked exactly the way Dakota had pictured him, except for the contented look in his eyes. Tall, dark and solemn, he was decidedly a man at peace with the world he found himself in. The right job, the right life. The right woman at his side.

It wasn't always so, but she had no way of knowing that. She envied him the moment she met him, wondering if that kind of tranquillity would ever be hers to enjoy.

Spotting him hadn't been difficult. His was the only pink Cadillac in the car rental lot as they drove up. He was standing beside it like a proud father silently basking in the glory of his offspring.

It took all kinds, Dakota thought. But as long as the man helped her get Vinny back, she didn't care if he rode a pet llama decked out in purple rigging to get to where he was going.

"I've only got a few minutes," Graham told them after Rusty had introduced Dakota and they all shook hands. Gray got down to business immediately. "One of Del Greco's men phones in daily orders by noon. Del Greco likes to keep everything nice and orderly," he explained when Dakota looked mildly surprised. "Superstitious that way. He shops at a place called Santini's Grocery."

It was Rusty's turn to look surprised. "Not a supermarket?" If nothing else, the variety there would be much broader, as would the anonymity.

It was another quirk they'd uncovered. "Del Greco likes the little man. In more ways than one. The little man is easier to fleece," he explained. "Easier to control and keep under his thumb. Del Greco's old-fashioned. He clings to the old rules in a modern world. What that boils down to is that he gets his money from protection and from silent partnerships—usually—in gambling establishments. No drugs, no prostitution."

"A regular Boy Scout," Dakota commented bitterly.

"He could be worse," Gray replied, but there was sympathy in his dark eyes.

"Not to me."

Rusty took in what was being said, but he was focusing on the immediate future, on finding a way to deliver the groceries into Del Greco's kitchen himself. "What can you tell me about Santini?"

Gray took out a sheet he'd printed up less than an hour ago.

"Way ahead of you. Here's a bio on the man in case anyone asks any questions." He handed Rusty the sheet. "You get in any trouble, call. Old-world principles or not, Del Greco and his organization are a nasty crew by anyone's standards. Don't play hero."

Rusty grinned, folding the paper and tucking it into his pocket. He thought of what Dakota had said to him in her apartment. She'd asked him to be her hero. "That's my job."

Gray didn't crack a smile. "Cemetery's full of dead heroes."

Rusty glanced at Dakota. "You two have a lot in common. Same sunny outlook."

"Better grim than dead," Gray told him. Just then, his beeper went off. Barely glancing at the number that flashed there, he muttered, "This is it."

"Breaking case?" Rusty asked as Gray hurriedly opened the door on the driver's side of his gleaming car. Though still composed, the man seemed to be just the slightest bit agitated.

"Breaking water," Gray corrected. He fumbled with his key, pushing it into the ignition. "My wife's just gone into labor."

His "Goodbye" and "Good luck" were swallowed up by the roar of his engine as he peeled out of the spot. The car's siren went on half a second later.

Rusty turned to Dakota. "Okay, let's trade this Smurf car in and then get back to the motel."

"The motel?" She took the steps up to the rental agency's front door. "Why can't we just get started?"

Reaching around Dakota, he pushed open the door for her. "We are started, but I'm going to need to pick up some extra equipment and see if Savannah's finished arranging for a vehicle for us yet."

That didn't make any sense to her. "If she's arranging for one, why are we bothering to exchange this one?"

"Because we need some practical wheels to travel around in." He lowered his voice so that the woman at the far end of the counter couldn't hear. "If we're going to hang around in Del Greco's vicinity, we need something that can be hidden in plain sight. Like a van from the cable company, or one of the utility companies."

She looked at her watch. Redhawk had said the orders were placed every day by noon. "Are we going to be able to get all this done before twelve o'clock?"

He gestured toward the counter. "We're going to damn well try."

The cell phone rang just as they pulled into the motel lot. The vehicle they were in was a midsize car with plenty of room for even someone of Rusty's height.

He looked at Dakota. "I guess I can get this one myself."

She pressed her lips together, trying not to think about the last call. "Yeah."

Angling so that he could reach the phone in his pocket, he pulled it out. "This is Rusty."

"Hey, Saint Rusty," Savannah greeted him on the other end, "believe it or not, we have a taker on that baby streetwalker whose photograph you e-mailed me last night. Took some sifting, but I finally found her on the Web site. I missed her the first time because she looked so well scrubbed in her photo. I called her parents—they live on a ranch in Montana—and told them where she was. The father cried incoherently for ten minutes. A Mr. Henry Bradford, in case you're wondering. Said that his daughter Lisa had been missing for almost six months. Ran off after an argument. He's planning on flying to Las Vegas to bring her home the minute he can get a flight out. Best Christmas present he ever had. Told me to bless you before he hung up. Consider yourself blessed."

A feeling of accomplishment surged through Rusty. One down, a million to go, but he'd made a difference, brought one shattered family together. There was no substitute for the feeling that was rushing through him. "I'll feel more blessed if you have a line on that vehicle I need."

"Already taken care of. Sam made a couple of calls," she told him. He could hear the smile in her voice as she mentioned her husband's name. "Know anything about hooking up cables?"

"Can a bird fly?"

"Not all of them," she reminded him. He was the youngest member of the agency, and since he'd come to work for them before he was even out of college, they all felt rather protective of him, a feeling she knew frustrated him at times. Still, it didn't keep her from saying, "Just be careful, you hear?"

"Yes, ma'am."

She gave him the location where he could find the truck. "This is a huge favor. The man who's lending you the truck is a friend of Sam's and he's going out on a limb. His supervisor's out of town until Monday. He's going to need the truck by then."

"No problem." He sincerely hoped that by the end of that time they'd have the information they needed. "Besides, after that, it gets to look too suspicious to have the same truck hanging around the area."

Savannah was well versed in the drill. Surveillance was the backbone of the job. "Let me know if you need another vehicle rounded up."

"You'll be the first to know," he promised with a laugh. "I'll be in touch."

"Be sure you are. Oh, and Rusty, Cade says to tell you, good work with that girl."

Cade was not stingy with his praise, but it was always nice to hear that his efforts were appreciated. "Tell him thanks." Rusty rang off, flipping the phone shut. Tucking it away, he looked at Dakota. "We've got—"

"The truck, I heard," she told him.

Because she'd been one once, she thought of the

runaway. The one he'd just helped. Except in her case, there would have been no loving parents to return to, no arms waiting to embrace her. Just the state, waiting to place her in yet another loveless setting. Dakota looked at Rusty. He'd put himself out for no reward other than the good deed itself. She'd stopped believing that people like him existed a long time ago.

"So that girl's parents are coming to get her?"

He nodded, getting out of the car. "I told you, we deal in happy endings."

She prayed that whatever luck he had held out a little longer. "I'm going to hold you to that." She closed the car door firmly.

He looked at her over the roof of the car. "I wouldn't have it any other way."

Every rule had an exception. Mentally, Rusty crossed his fingers that this case wouldn't turn out to be the exception.

But he knew he wouldn't let it, because no matter what it took, even if her son wasn't physically at Del Greco's Las Vegas estate, as long as he had some clue that Del Greco did have the boy, he was going to find Vinny for her. He wasn't about to give up until he saw Dakota holding her son in her arms.

It was a promise that went beyond the verbal contract he'd given her when she'd come to the agency. It was a commitment he made to every case he worked on. And never so fiercely as the one he made now, to her.

The smile on her lips was sad. "You know, I almost believe you."

He tried to not be swayed by the sadness he saw in her eyes, struggled against the desire to take her into his arms and just hold her, just comfort her. She'd only take it as a come-on, not what it was. One human being reaching out to another.

Besides, he thought, maybe she was right. Because what he was feeling wasn't completely altruistic.

He was going to have to watch that.

"Good." He unlocked the motel door. "Like I said, keep working on that trusting thing. You'll get it down pat yet."

Chapter 11

The delivery truck driver, Sonny, according to the name stitched in white just beneath the Santini's logo on his navy-blue shirt, eyed the hundred-dollar bill Rusty was holding out to him the way a starving dog eyed a sirloin steak that was just out of reach.

Dakota could almost see the man literally drool at the bill. Barely out of his teens, if that old, the hundred had to seem like a great deal of money to him.

Still, the driver slowly shook his dark head, torn and uncertain which way to go.

Sonny scratched his head, as if the moral dilemma he was contemplating was just too much for him to handle.

"I dunno, I dunno." He repeated the phrase like a mantra.

At exactly twelve noon, the tall, strapping grocery store errand boy had loaded Santini's small delivery truck at the rear of the store and left the premises. Tailing him to make sure of his destination, Rusty had pulled his newly rented car in front of the truck less than three miles away from Del Greco's compound.

Sonny had leaned out the window, shouting obscenities, his temper flaring. His temper was extinguished as soon as he saw Rusty get out of the car and walk toward him. When he was told to step out of the vehicle, Sonny only gripped the steering wheel harder and cowered. However, seeing Dakota approaching behind Rusty, the request to step out of the vehicle had suddenly seemed less like a threat and more like an invitation.

The offer of money was made quickly and succinctly, but it seemed to sail right over the younger man's head. His IQ appeared to be only a little larger than his shoe size.

Sonny stood now, shifting from foot to foot, clearly undecided and just as clearly tempted. His dark eyes slanted toward Rusty. "Tell me again why you want to take my place and deliver the groceries?"

In a quiet, calm voice, Rusty repeated what he'd said only minutes before. "Mr. Del Greco's my uncle and I'm just playing a trick on him."

Sonny chewed on a near-nonexistent lower lip. "I don't know. Mr. Del Greco and the others, they're very particular about who comes in and out." A thought appeared suddenly to strike him and he looked as if the force of the blow might knock him down. "You could be a policeman or something."

He looked from Rusty to Dakota nervously. "And then Mr. Del Greco would get real mad. He might even—"

Rusty was quick to cut in. "Do I look crazy to you? Do I?" he pressed.

"Um, no." Sonny stared at him, trying to discern whether he'd answered correctly.

Still holding the hundred aloft, Rusty slipped a conspiratorial arm around the younger man's shoulders.

"Hey, I know what my uncle does for a living. If I weren't his nephew, do you think I'd be stupid enough just to waltz right in there, unprotected? Without a hundred guys right behind me? My uncle's 'associates' would cut me down in a heartbeat."

The explanation seemed to make sense to Sonny. Or maybe the temptation of the hundred had won out over what little common sense the young man possessed. In any event, he nodded his head vigorously in agreement.

"Okay, but this won't take long, will it? I gotta have the truck back pretty quick. Mr. Santini's got a temper, too. I don't like it when he yells at me."

"Not long," Rusty promised, relieved that he had won the driver over so easily. "I'll just be in and out, have a laugh with the old man and be back before you know it." He indicated Dakota. "You can even stay with my girlfriend for collateral."

Dakota's mouth dropped open in surprise, but the protest she was about to make at being called his girlfriend faded. Whatever it took to get Vinny back, she was willing to do. Even baby-sit a wisdom-challenged delivery truck driver.

Sonny's muddy eyes brightened as he looked at Dakota. That cinched the deal for him.

"Okay." He plucked the hundred from Rusty's hand and shoved it happily into his pants' pocket.

Rusty took hold of his arm. "Get in the truck, I need to change clothes with you."

Sonny was instantly horrified, afraid that he had somehow made a huge mistake. "Hey, wait a minute, you didn't say nothing about taking off no clothes. I don't do that kind of stuff with men."

Rusty bit back his impatience. Out of the corner of his eye, he could see Dakota struggling to not laugh. "Neither do I," Rusty assured him. "But I have to switch clothes with you. Otherwise, they're going to know that I'm not from Santini's and the joke's over before it even starts."

Sonny pursed his lips, thinking. His eyes squinted from the effort. He glanced over again at Dakota. "All right, I guess."

Ten minutes later Rusty was behind the wheel of Santini's Grocery's delivery truck, dressed in Sonny's navy-blue shirt and khaki pants and driving toward the Del Greco compound. He waved at Dakota just before taking the turn that led him down the hillside.

Dakota sat in the rental car, her heart in her mouth. The light beige car was parked behind a row of trees that hid it from the view of anyone who looked up from the estate. She watched the truck grow smaller and smaller before it finally disappeared behind towering, black wrought-iron gates. She could just barely make out a guard in a booth just to the right of the entrance.

Though she didn't want to think about it, she had a bad feeling about the venture.

The bad feeling grew as time ticked away.

It didn't help matters any that the delivery boy was sitting next to her and keeping up a stream of nonstop chatter that was swiftly driving her crazy. Occasionally, she offered monosyllabic answers when he paused to suck in a breath, saying "So, what do you think?"

Every few minutes she glanced at her watch, then at the clock on the dashboard to make sure her watch hadn't stopped. Her stomach began to tighten as her anxiety continued to escalate.

Too much time had lapsed.

Just how long did it take to plant a damn surveillance device? It had to be less time than had gone by, she reasoned. Fifteen minutes had ticked away since the grocery truck had disappeared from view.

Was he even still alive?

She resisted the urge to chew on her nails. Beside her, Sonny droned on. Something about an exciting experience on his prom night. She had a feeling that, left unchecked, he could go on this way indefinitely, recounting every event in his life. She stopped even making token answers.

What if the men inside saw through Andreini's story? What if they didn't believe that Sonny had taken half a sick day and that he was subbing for the younger man? What if they saw him plant one of the surveillance devices?

He'd be dead before his fingers had a chance to leave the bug.

A chill ran down her back as fragments of scenarios continued to suggest themselves to her.

She'd read accounts of Del Greco in the newspaper after she'd found out that he was Vincent's father, accounts that had made her blood run cold. The small, gray-haired man with the aristocratic hands and gentle smile could order the systematic wiping out of an entire family while eating a fine gourmet meal without so much as pausing for a heartbeat.

What if Del Greco was ordering Andreini killed while she sat here thinking?

It would be her fault, all her fault. She couldn't just sit here like this any longer, waiting to see if Andreini returned. If he was in trouble, she had to do something to help him.

The best way was to create a diversion. Dakota made up her mind. She was going down to the house. Once she reached it, it was anyone's guess what she was going to do. She only hoped an idea would hit her between now and five minutes from now.

"Hey, lady, what are you doing?" Sonny suddenly halted his narrative midsentence as Dakota turned the key in the ignition. His eyes brightened. "Are we going somewhere? You know, Mr. Santini doesn't like it if I take too long. Of course, if a honey like you's involved, he'll understand. Maybe," he added nervously, his Adam's apple dancing up and down his throat.

She'd had just about all she could take. "Number one, I'm not a honey. Number two, will you please just sit still and shut up?"

"Hey!" Sonny protested indignantly, his voice cracking just enough to embarrass him. "I didn't come looking for you, you guys came to me, and—"

The door on the driver's side suddenly opened. Dakota jumped, her fist pulled back. She curtailed her punch just in time.

"Omigod, you're all right." With a cry of relief, she bounced out of the car and threw her arms around Rusty. "You're alive." Without thinking, only reacting, she kissed him soundly on the lips.

To say that he was surprised would be one of the great understatements of the decade. But Rusty always knew how to rise to an occasion and this time was no exception. Slipping his arms around the warm, supple body that was pressed against his, he let the kiss happen, absorbed her feverish embrace as his due after having survived a walk through the lion's den. For a moment there he hadn't been altogether sure that he would.

Maybe if Del Greco's capo hadn't been inherently lazy, he might have been forced to undergo closer scrutiny after he'd given his story about Sonny getting sick. When the other man had challenged him, Rusty had offered to leave the groceries on the doorstep if he was under some kind of suspicion.

Didn't make any difference to him, he'd said to the

capo. The pay was the same. Del Greco's first-in-command had waved him into the kitchen, telling him to unpack the groceries and be quick about it.

When he'd folded up the bags and put them away where he was told, Rusty had finally found the opportunity to plant one of the tiny, state-of-the-art surveillance chips that were part of Megan's bag of tricks and that would allow them to both see and hear what was going on in that part of the Del Greco house. Stopping to tie his undone shoelace in the living room had allowed him to plant the other on the leg of an antique table.

That done, though he moved slowly in keeping with his laid-back, lazy image, he couldn't get out of the house fast enough. Dakota's unexpected greeting was just icing on the cake.

The kiss was deepening, sucking her into it. And Dakota was going willingly. Tantalized, for a moment she almost allowed it to continue. But then she came to what was left of her senses.

What was she *doing?*

She realized that stress had pushed her over the brink. Why else was she passionately kissing a man she hardly knew?

She'd let her emotions get the better of her. Big mistake. Backing up, she looked at him and flushed.

"Sorry."

Sonny, looking on with intense envy and vicariously enjoying the ride, scratched his head, puzzled by her abrupt change of direction.

"Why is your girlfriend apologizing for kissing you?"

"Long story." Blowing out a breath as he tried to catch his bearings, Rusty clapped his hand over the delivery boy's shoulder. "C'mon, let's get you back into your own clothes and on your way before your boss starts getting suspicious."

The call to reality did the trick, although Sonny looked rather reluctant to call an end to the charade. With a sigh, he allowed himself to be herded away.

Ten minutes later, with an extra hundred dollars in his pocket to insure that this little episode was "just between them," Sonny drove the delivery truck away. He paused only once to look longingly over his shoulder at Dakota.

For the second time that day Dakota felt as if she were ready to climb out of her skin. Waiting until the driver was out of sight was driving her crazy.

"Did you see him?" she demanded the second Sonny was down the road. "Did you see Vinny? Is he on the compound?"

Rusty shook his head. "I didn't see him. I didn't even get a chance to see the head man." If Del Greco was present in the house, he had been nowhere in sight. "If your son's there, most probably Del Greco has him in one of the upstairs rooms." He looked at her. There were tiny lines on her forehead where her brow had furrowed. He fought the urge to smooth them out with his fingers. He thought of the way she'd greeted him. "Were you worried about me?"

She shrugged, looking away, upbraiding herself for

having lost control like that. But it had been such a relief to see that he was still alive and that she wasn't responsible for his demise. "You took a long time, I didn't know what to think."

To him, time had raced by while he'd been in the compound. "Planting bugs isn't like sticking on postage stamps."

"I know," she snapped curtly. "It's just that..." She saw the amused look on his face and damned him for it. "I didn't want your blood on my conscience, all right?" Uncomfortable with the way he was looking at her and the way she was reacting to him, she shifted the focus of the conversation. "Besides, if I'd had to sit here listening to that mindless dolt try to seduce me one more second, I was going to be the one committing murder."

"He tried to seduce you?" Not that, of course, he could blame Sonny. In any case, he judged that Dakota was more than the younger man's match.

She laughed shortly. "Did everything but get out and perform a tribal mating dance around the car, preening like a peacock."

Rusty got into the vehicle, waiting for Dakota to come around to her side.

"That's what you get for being gorgeous." He started the car. They had to hide this one and bring out the cable truck. "A kid with his hormones at peak running order can't be held responsible for behaving like an idiot in heat around someone who looks the way you do."

She pulled her seat belt into place, frowning at his description. "Am I supposed to be flattered?"

If he was going to flatter her, he would have used far more flowery language than that. "No, just understanding. Men tend to act like fools when their brains go into meltdown."

"Yours hasn't." The moment the words were out, she cursed herself. She had absolutely no idea what had made her say that.

The smile that slipped over his face as he slanted a look at her was nothing short of sexy. Dakota felt it clear down to the bone. "I've got a job to do. Catch me once this is over and I'll show you what a brain in meltdown looks like."

Her throat suddenly felt dry. She decided that her own brain had to have suffered a temporary meltdown of its own, otherwise, there was no plausible explanation for why she said, "Maybe I will." Embarrassed by the unguarded slip, she nodded toward the house. "Are you sure those devices work?"

He tested them on a regular basis, as he did all the equipment left in his care. "Only one way to find out."

He surprised her by stopping the car. Getting out, Rusty went to the trunk and opened it. He leaned in and did some adjusting to the surveillance receivers before turning it on slowly.

From the device he'd planted in the kitchen, there was nothing. The area was empty. But there were both voices and images coming in from the device he'd planted in the living room. He could make out both Del Greco's head of security and one of his soldiers discussing the merits of a showgirl both men seemed to know in the absolute sense of the word.

Rusty smiled at Dakota as he gestured toward the small screen. "Houston, we have liftoff."

They switched cars, situating the cable truck where the rental car had previously been. It was the last thing done quickly.

The rest of the day was spent straining to hear the sounds of a childish voice, or to catch a glimpse of a small boy hurrying through one of the two rooms. Neither happened. People came and went, voices changed, but none belonged to a small boy.

Dakota began to feel that Rusty's effort had been both hopeless and useless.

"Look, maybe if we just sneak onto the property after everyone's in bed..."

Patience was always the last thing to go for him. He still had enough to gently point out, "You're just being punchy." Shifting in the crammed interior, he rotated his shoulders. As everything else, they felt stiff. "Security's too tight. A spider doesn't stand a chance of sneaking in without being detected."

He was right and she hated him for it. "Well, we just can't sit here," she insisted.

"Yes," he told her, his quiet voice firm, "we can. We can sit here and watch and wait. Sooner or later, if Vinny's staying there, he's got to use the front door or the back door. And then we'll see him. There's no helicopter landing pad on the roof, no other way in or out of the house. If your son's there," he assured her, "we'll see him."

She shrugged, knowing he was right. Knowing her reaction was born out of frustration and irritation. She was tired of waiting, tied of worrying. Tired of running. Dakota closed her eyes, exhausted. Every bone in her body ached. "You know, these chairs aren't exactly the last word in comfort."

"Best they could do on short notice."

Her eyes opened and she looked at him accusingly. "Do you always have to be so damn cheerful and logical?" she snapped.

"Don't see much point in losing my temper." He fined-tuned one of the monitors that had temporarily become fuzzy. "I pick my battles."

"Meaning I should pick mine?"

She sounded as if she just had. He held up his hand. "No, meaning that—"

But she'd raised her own hand to silence him. Alert, she'd picked up the sound of a new voice coming from the transmitter in the living room. A smooth, cultured voice. She'd only been in the man's presence twice, but he had left an indelible impression. One that haunted her worst nightmares.

"Del Greco." Dakota indicated the image on the black-and-white screen.

The small, thin man carried himself with dignity, like the unchallenged ruler of an empire. But the emperor was old. And frail.

Sitting up straight, Dakota scrutinized the image, scanning the area around him.

There was no sign of her son.

She felt as if her heart was constricting within her chest.

Del Greco was talking to one of his chief soldiers, asking him something about the pending arrival of a package. Package. Was that some code word he was using for Vinny?

She grabbed Rusty's wrist as she listened. And prayed. The harder she prayed, the harder she squeezed his wrist, her nails digging into his flesh. She was oblivious to everything but the sound of Del Greco's voice.

Finally, the man went out of range and the camera went dormant. Del Greco had said absolutely nothing to enlighten them.

They were no better off than before.

Dakota sighed, falling back like an inflated doll that suddenly had all the air siphoned out of it. Hysteria began clawing at her, threatening to break loose. She squeezed her eyes shut to keep any tears from seeping out.

Her voice was shaky. "I don't know how much more of this I can take."

"Yeah, you do," Rusty contradicted. Dakota opened her eyes to look at him. "You'll take it until we find Vinny. You're a lot stronger than you think, you know."

She didn't feel very strong right now. She felt weary. Weary clear down to the bone. Maybe even further than that. "Is that part of your pep talk?"

"No, just part of the instincts you're paying me

for.'' He continued to watch the living-room monitor. But there was nothing. It appeared that the key players were calling it a night.

''I thought I was paying you to find my son.''

''That, too.'' Rusty glanced at his watch. It was almost ten. ''Why don't we call it a night?'' He saw resistance rise in her eyes. ''There's no reason for a cable truck to be here this late. Not with what overtime costs these days. If anyone's noticed the truck, it'll look less suspicious if we leave now and come back tomorrow.''

She wanted to protest, to say that they were staying right where they were until they saw something that they could work with. Something that would lead them to Vinny. They were so close, damn it, so very close. Why was this dragging out this way?

And she didn't know if he was right in his assessment of her, though she wanted him to be. She didn't know how strong she was. She had had so many hard knocks in her life, but this one was the worst of all to bear. It was the one that could finally break her.

She wanted to insist that they weren't moving from this spot, but she knew that Andreini was right. They couldn't afford to arouse suspicion.

With a sigh, she climbed from the back to the front of the truck and slid into the passenger seat.

''You're not going to try to make me eat something, are you?''

In the driver's seat, Rusty started up the truck. ''Lady, even would-be heroes have their limits. I wouldn't try to make you do anything.''

She had her doubts about that.

But for the sake of argument, she nodded her head, watching the compound in the distance grow smaller and smaller in her side mirror. ''As long as we understand each other,'' she murmured.

Not yet, he thought, but he was working on it.

Chapter 12

Despair didn't actually hit Dakota until she walked back into the motel room. And then it leaped out at her, attacking with a vengeance, ripping into her heart and making her bleed.

Walking in ahead of Rusty, Dakota switched on the light. The first thing she saw was Vinny's beloved stuffed bear sitting on the bed, drooping forlornly against the pillows where she'd left it.

Though she struggled against it, emotion overwhelmed her like an unruly tidal wave determined to steal the very breath out of her and smother her.

Her eyes instantly filled with tears. The next moment they were spilling out despite her determination to keep them back.

Biting her lower lip did nothing to quell the sudden break in control or to curtail the flow of tears. They ran freely down her cheeks. The dam had broken and all she was left with were pieces, pieces that felt as if they were shattered beyond repair.

With her last ounce of strength, Dakota let out a slow, shaky breath, hoping the man walking into the room behind her wouldn't notice that she'd suddenly begun falling apart. She desperately needed some time to pull herself together.

She should have known better. She was paying him to notice everything.

''Dakota?''

Keeping her back to Rusty, she raised her hand, waving him away. Willing him to obey. When she felt his hands gently take possession of her shoulders, she wanted to lash out at him, to yell, to scream. To tell him to back off in no uncertain terms.

But no words came.

There was this huge lump in her throat, a lump too large to allow anything to get through. A lump that threatened to choke her.

Rusty turned her around slowly, his hold on her gentle but firm. Valiantly, she kept her head down and to the side, wanting him to take the hint and to just leave her alone. But he lifted her chin, forcing her to look up at him.

She hated him for it. Hated him for seeing her crumble this way.

The second they had walked into the room, he had detected the change in her. The gladiator armor she kept so close to her body just seemed to collapse. He perceived it in the way her shoulders sagged and knew she was crying without even having to look at her face. He read it in her body language.

When he finally succeeded in making her look up at him, the sight of her tears twisted his heart, squeezing it. Though he knew she would resist the contact, Rusty took her into his arms anyway and kissed the top of her head. She needed to be held.

''We'll get him back,'' he promised her softly.

He felt her quietly crying against him, her anguish making any response momentarily impossible. When she managed to pull herself together enough to be coherent, she clung to him as if he was all that stood between her and utter hopelessness.

''It's almost Christmas.'' She'd wanted to give Vinny a wonderful Christmas full of presents and laughter. They were supposed to have gone out together to get a tree. Instead, he'd been snatched away and she was playing hide-and-seek with a crime kingpin who could, at any given moment, make the separation permanent.

Rusty's arms tightened around her. ''He'll be home for Christmas.''

Suddenly, anger, the ever-protective shield she'd always reached for, always hidden behind, flared within her. ''How can you promise me that?'' she demanded hotly.

It wasn't Dakota talking, it was her desperation. He knew that. Rusty took her face in his hands and looked into her eyes. Willing her to believe the promise he meant to keep.

''Because I can.'' His voice was firm. ''Because

it's true. No matter what it takes, I promise you your son will be home for Christmas.''

She knew she was a fool for believing him, and yet she needed so much to believe. Needed so much to trust this man who had come into her life uninvited, taking on her trouble as his own. Dakota sobbed, burying her face in his chest again, holding on to him tightly. As tightly as she was holding on to his words.

''I'm sorry. I'm not usually like this. I'm *never* like this,'' she amended, her voice hitching in the middle. ''I can't remember the last time I cried this much.''

She'd even remained dry-eyed at Vincent's funeral. She'd heard his father call her names, but she'd been too numbed to cry, trying to make some kind of plans for her baby now that she found herself alone. There weren't many calls for pregnant showgirls well along in their sixth month.

''That's okay. Under the circumstances, tears are allowed.'' Moved by the vulnerability in her eyes, Rusty kissed her forehead. ''I won't tell anyone. Detective-client privilege,'' he informed her with a smile, fervently wishing there was some way he could cut through all the obstacles and bring the boy to her side.

But they still didn't even know if Vinny was at the compound. Even if Gray could somehow come up with a search warrant to look for the boy on the estate, Rusty knew that there was no telling whether Del Greco was keeping his grandson on the premises or had had him shifted to one of his other houses in the country. For that matter, they still weren't a hundred percent certain that Del Greco'd had the boy abducted. They needed more input and he couldn't get it for her fast enough. Yet.

Dakota looked up, the soft comfort of his kiss seeping into her, warming her. Stirring her. Tears marking a fresh, damp trail along her cheeks, she tilted her head upward and sought his lips.

The reaction caught him off guard. Pleasure came immediately, like a burst of sunlight. Rusty meant only to brush his lips against hers, to offer the same comfort he'd already attempted to give.

But the touch of her mouth to his ignited the fire in his belly that had been patiently dormant ever since he'd first kissed her. The fire that had begun the very first time he had laid eyes on her as she'd hurried by, her hand firmly wrapped around her child's small fingers.

A man could live for a week on the fantasies her kiss generated.

Without conscious thought, Rusty tightened his arms around her even further, felt her body lean into his as the kiss deepened of its own accord. It was as if everything had suddenly launched into automatic pilot.

The road ahead promised to be a bumpy one.

Knowing that this time, if he let things go any further, he might not be able to break away as he had the last time, Rusty pulled back and looked down into her face.

He wanted her.

But what he didn't want was for remorse to be the

first reaction to their lovemaking. It was bad enough that it would come later.

"Dakota—"

She could see the words that were coming. There was a noble look in his eye, the kind of look a man had when he was about to make a sacrifice.

She didn't want a sacrifice, not tonight. She wanted to forget, forget everything, the pain, the uncertainty, the threat of what life would be like if she didn't get her son back. For the duration of the night, she wanted to not think at all.

Raising her fingers to his lips, she stopped their movement. "Don't talk, Andreini. Just make love with me. To me," she added, her voice low, soft, and almost supplicant.

She was about to make a mistake, and if he wasn't careful, he was going to help her. He tried to hold her at arm's length and couldn't quite get himself to manage it. "You're overwrought, Dakota. You don't know what you're saying."

She shook her head. Didn't he understand? She *needed* this. Needed him.

"Yes, I do. I'm saying that I want you to make this pain go away for a little while. I can hardly breathe, it's so bad." Her eyes searched his face for the understanding she had come, in such a short while, to know he possessed. "Please, Rusty, help me."

It was the first time she'd ever called him by anything but his surname. Rusty felt his resolve snapping. He knew he should back away from her, from the temptation she represented. Knew he should tuck her into bed and go out for a long walk in the night air until it cleared away the vapors from his brain and cooled the hot blood surging in his veins.

But he didn't go. He stayed just where he was. He had no choice.

Cupping her face, he stayed and kissed her. Kissed her and consequently lost himself in her the way a man running through a lush, hot jungle loses himself.

There were no markers for him to find his way out, no noble stance to take even though he knew he was breaking every damn rule he'd ever set down for himself, not to mention some that were probably on the books in the agency.

He didn't care. She tasted like sweet, forbidden fruit, and he didn't care.

Rusty couldn't help himself. He didn't seem to have the self-control he normally possessed. Not with her request echoing in his brain and the taste of her mouth on his.

His body heated and he picked her up into his arms, his mouth never leaving hers. Gently, Rusty placed her on the bed.

The stuffed animal that had initiated the sudden loss of control fell by the wayside as it tumbled from the bed onto the floor.

Lying down beside her, Rusty kissed her over and over again. Her lips, her neck, her face. With each pass, the intensity grew until he felt it was almost savage.

Like a woman possessed, Dakota kissed him everywhere, nipping on his mouth, tracing delicate lines along his throat, his face. No longer held in check, she seemed to have suddenly become frenzied.

The thought came slamming home to him. He had to rise above his own desires, his own demanding passion and think of her, he upbraided himself urgently. He needed to back away.

Rusty caught her hands as her fingers swiftly moved to undo the buttons on his shirt. She looked at him, dazed, bewildered.

"What?"

His body throbbing, his loins yearning for release, for her, he'd never exercised as much rigid control as he did at this moment.

"Dakota, stop." She tried to pull her hands out of his grip. "You're going to regret this."

Maybe later, but not now. Now she needed to be held, to be made mindless, just a mass of pulsating needs, and she knew he could do that for her. *Was* doing that for her. But he couldn't stop.

"Don't talk," she begged. "Please."

The last of his resolve, shredded as it was, broke apart completely. The attraction he had felt from the very start flourished, completely engulfing him. There was no turning back.

He wasn't nearly as noble as he would have liked to believe.

The fire in his belly spread, consuming all of him. He literally felt as if he burned for her. He'd always thought that was a ridiculous phrase. People didn't burn, they wanted.

Yet he burned. And only she could put out the fire.

But he quickly learned that she couldn't. With each passing moment, as he touched her, as he fondled and possessed her, he discovered that she could only make the fire grow hotter.

With each response, with every movement of her body, her hands, her lips, she made the fire grow within him.

More than anything, Rusty didn't want to take her like some rutting animal. He wanted this to be wonderful for her. For him. Yet it took every fiber of his being to prolong the process, especially when she seemed so very willing to bring him to a swift climax if only he would do the same for her.

Her hands tore at his clothes, pulling them urgently from his body as her body twisted and turned beneath his. A silent invitation was issued with each movement. Pure temptation. But there was nothing pure about the feelings he was having.

To prolong Dakota's pleasure, he teased her out of her clothes, first her blouse, then her jeans, although he wasn't sure just where he found the strength to hold back. When he pulled off her undergarments, his breathing quickened. Only his pulse outraced it.

Her unadorned body was just the way he'd envisioned it. Perfect. Skin like warm cream with just the vaguest touch of Kahlúa to it to give it vibrant color.

Unable to help himself, feeling as if he was in the presence of something truly wondrous, he feasted on Dakota's skin. Rusty kissed every inch of her body and gloried in the way she moved and moaned beneath him.

His body pulsed, begging for the final moment.

But she had begged him to make her forget, and he was bound and determined to keep his silent promise to her, just as he was going to keep the one he had uttered.

He wanted, most of all, to minimize the regret he knew she would feel once the urgency, the need to not think, had left her. He wanted her pleasure to outweigh any feelings of remorse. Or at least to balance it out.

Dakota could feel his mouth questing over her body. And then she could hardly catch her breath as he suddenly swept her over the first huge crest. The explosion rocked her body so that she heard herself whimpering.

Before she could reach for him, to attempt to match him sensation for sensation, another climax, different from the first, took her. And then, a delicious eternity later, when it faded, leaving her exhausted, she fell back, too limp to move.

Or so she thought until he began weaving the frantic magic around her again.

Usually she was the one who conjured, who was versed in the ins and outs of creating the ultimate pleasure. The lovers she'd had had come to her with preconceived notions of what a woman like her could do, and all she needed was to put only a part of herself into the act and that was enough for them.

But this time she was not the active force, the dominant one. This gentle, caring man who was determined to vanquish her despair, was playing her body as if she were some instrument that he had been dedicated to studying.

As his lips trailed toward her belly, Dakota caught his face with both her hands and dragged Rusty's mouth back up to hers.

"Now," she implored, or maybe only thought that she did. Maybe the word had only echoed in her head.

She felt Rusty's smile as it moved along his lips, felt it infiltrate her body as he brought his mouth to hers. Her body moved urgently beneath his, sealing both their fates.

"You are beautiful," he groaned.

"Talk is cheap," she rasped against his mouth. "I'm from Missouri. Show me."

She raised her hips to his in silent invitation. He gathered her against him as he slid into her. Linking them together for all time.

He began to move.

Dakota sank her nails into his back as the movements increased in tempo. He moved faster and faster, his eyes on hers, bringing them both to where they needed and wanted to be.

The rush began to take hold of her. Dakota wrapped her legs around his, pulling him further into her, never wanting the moment to end.

The moment came and Dakota held her breath as she absorbed it. The surge made her cry out his name against his mouth.

Rusty felt the euphoria grab hold of him and

tighten its fingers around him, just as Dakota tightened her legs around his.

He wanted to freeze time and hold this moment in the palm of his hand forever. Or at least to brand it upon his brain. He knew he wouldn't forget it for a long, long time.

Gently rolling off her, he gathered Dakota to him and held her as closely, as tightly, as he dared. She curled against him like a child seeking shelter from a storm. He felt something stir within him again, but this time he knew it wasn't just desire.

Rusty kissed the top of her head, a feeling of intimacy filling every small space within him. He knew he had no right to it, to this feeling. That what had happened here was just an isolated episode between two people who needed each other. But for the moment, he allowed himself to enjoy it while it lasted.

He loved the smell of her hair, he realized, the light scent of floral shampoo teasing his senses. Damn, but he could so easily grow accustomed to this feeling.

"Are you all right?" he murmured against her hair.

There was a haze clouding her brain, and a small blanket of contentment she was trying valiantly to hold to her. Contentment of the sort that she hadn't felt in a very long time.

She turned her face toward his, certain she hadn't heard correctly.

"What?"

"Are you all right?" he repeated. He looked down at her face, resisting the desire to kiss her again. He didn't want her to think that this was only about sex, even though the urgency was beginning to rise within him again. "I didn't hurt you, did I?"

"Hurt me?" Was he actually worried about how she felt? That he'd been too rough with her at the end? The idea stunned her. She'd never had a man concerned about hurting her before. Or even worried about her feelings. Even Vincent had been a lot more interested in reaching his own climax than in her mutual enjoyment, much less worried that she'd somehow suffered because of it. "How?"

Though he was gregarious, Rusty knew he didn't have a knack for wording things well when he most wanted to. When his heart was involved.

He tried again, lightly toying with the wisps of stray hair at her temple. "I mean, I wasn't too rough, was I?"

Was he serious? He'd been so gentle, she'd wanted to scream, "Faster." Dakota had trouble suppressing a laugh. "No, you weren't too rough."

Was her voice quavering? Was she trying to hold back a sob?

"Look, I know you're going to regret this." He searched for the right words. In lieu of them, he told her what was in his heart. "For what it's worth, I've never done this before."

Dakota couldn't resist going for the obvious interpretation and teasing him. This felt so different from all the other times she'd made love. She felt almost instantly comfortable.

There was a danger in that, in allowing herself to

relax, and she knew it, but she'd explore it all later, when the contentment faded.

For now she just wanted to be able to enjoy it. It was little enough to ask.

"You've never slept with a woman?" Her fingers swept over his chest, lightly outlining the hard pectoral muscles. She felt them tighten beneath her touch. "For a first-timer, you were very, very good."

"No. I mean, I don't sleep with clients." Rusty knew she knew he hadn't meant that he'd never slept with a woman before and that she was just enjoying herself. Still, he couldn't help voicing the question that rose to his lips. "How was I as someone who wasn't a first-timer?"

She smiled, her eyes crinkling, her body feeling incredibly mellow. There was no need to stretch the truth here. "Very, very good."

Her low, husky voice tantalized him. Aroused him. He traced her smile with his fingertips, wanting her so badly he felt his breath being stolen away. "That looks nice on you."

"What does?" she breathed, lightly kissing each of his fingers as they passed her lips. She saw desire flare in his eyes and felt a measure of triumph. And more than a little stirred.

"A smile. Makes you look softer, less ready for a fight."

She liked his honesty. Found it sexy. Found him even more so. She ran the tip of her tongue along her lips. Tasting him. Wanting him.

"I don't feel much like fighting right now."

He propped himself up on his elbow, looking down into her face. "What do you feel like doing?"

She moved closer to him, turning her body so that it tantalized his again. "Guess."

He tasted the smile he'd touted only moments ago as he kissed her again with all the passion he felt.

Chapter 13

The place beside him on the bed was empty. The sensation of warm emptiness registered quickly, banishing the formless haze that sleep had brought with it. Instantly alert because of the change, Rusty opened his eyes as he propped himself up on his elbow.

He saw her standing by the bureau, slipping into her shoes. He took a second to admire the graceful curve of her legs, the same legs that had been wrapped around him hours earlier.

The ray of euphoria created by the memory made him smile. "Good morning."

The sound of his voice surprised her. She'd thought he was asleep, which was why she'd hurried into her clothes rather than linger the way she wanted to. If she'd lingered beside him, temptation might have gotten the better of her. And that would be a bad thing.

The light of day shone on her mistake. Last night shouldn't have happened. But it had and she had to make the best of it.

Dakota didn't waste time with pleasantries. Straightening her blouse, she glanced at his reflection in the mirror rather than turn around and face him. "We have to get moving."

He took his cue from her voice and from her rigid body language. Somehow, they had returned to the first square they had ever occupied. Scrubbing a hand over his face, trying to engage his brain, he looked out the window. Daylight had made its appearance.

"What time is it?"

"Almost seven." Still using the mirror as a buffer, she felt her heart quicken at the sight of his body as he got out of bed.

Stop it, damn it. What the hell's wrong with you? He's just a man.

The silent, stern upbraiding echoed in her brain. The latter, however, wasn't quite the master of her body just yet. But she'd work on it. She knew better than to let herself be sidetracked this way.

Dakota stared at a cracked corner of the mirror, deliberately averting her eyes from the heart-stopping specimen of unselfconscious, naked manliness reflected in front of her and existing behind her. She pressed her fingers into the bureau surface until she could feel the imprint of the years of accumulated scars beneath them.

Move.

She grabbed the brush she'd hastily thrown into her

purse and began to pull it through her hair with more feeling than skill. She heard the rustling of sheets, like someone looking for his clothes. Her cheeks felt warmer, threatening to turn a deep shade of pink.

She had to set things straight.

"Look, I don't want you getting the wrong idea about last night." Her tone was detached. "I mean, it was nice, but it didn't mean anything."

Her words were like tiny razors, slashing away at him, trying to score a flesh wound. "You can only speak for yourself."

Checking in the mirror to assure herself that he at least had his jeans on, she swung around to face the man who had all but stopped the world for her last night. But things happened in the night, she told herself, that couldn't stand up to the light of day.

"Right, and from experience."

He said nothing for a long moment as he studied her face, her eyes. And then Rusty smiled ever so slightly. "I don't think you've run up against anyone like me before."

Her chin shot up and she gave him the best haughty look she had in her arsenal. "That's rather vain, don't you think?"

"No, just truthful." Finding his shirt, the one with the cable company's logo stitched over the pocket, he shrugged into it. "And observant."

They looked like mismatched characters out of some bizarre play, she thought. His outfit mirrored hers. Part of the charade they were trying to perpetuate. "What is that supposed to mean?"

He looked at her significantly, wishing that he could read her thoughts and in the process erase all the bad things that had scarred her. "If you'd run into men who treated you like you were something other than an incredibly beautiful woman, you wouldn't react this way now."

Exasperation flared. How dare he stand there, analyzing her? He was just handing her a line, anyway. All men did.

She wasn't about to waste any more time discussing this. Not now while her baby needed her. Not ever, she amended. She tossed the brush onto the bureau. "Let's go. We can get something to eat on the way."

Rusty tucked in his shirt. Maybe it was best if things just simmered awhile. Last night had been too hot for things not to cool down a bit, at least marginally. No woman had ever made him feel like a volcano before, about to erupt over and over again. He needed to put a few things into perspective himself.

Opening the door, he gestured her out. "After you."

Dakota said nothing as she passed him.

They drove the cable truck to a place not too far from where they had previously parked it. Rusty felt that the slight switch was just enough to not arouse suspicion. Repairs on cable lines were known to go on for a matter of days, if necessary, to eradicate any problems in a system. The lines in this area, Rusty had been briefed, were old and all needed replacing.

The cable company's budget didn't allow for wholesale renovation, so repairs were made as the need arose.

At most he figured that gave them another two days to find a clue as to Vinny's actual whereabouts. He needn't have bothered with his calculations.

Holding up the two bags of fast-food breakfast they'd picked up on the way, he gave Dakota her choice. "You want your indigestion fast, or slow?"

"Fast. I like to get things over with."

He smiled, handing her the left bag. "That wasn't the impression I got last night, at least, not the second time around."

Her eyes darkened. "I told you—"

Suddenly the truck's rear doors were yanked open, revealing blinding sunlight. And a handgun.

"Andreini," Dakota shouted as light bounced off the silver muzzle of the weapon held by a man who all but filled the entire space. Because the sun was directly behind him, it was almost impossible to see anything else.

She didn't have to see. She knew.

Dakota dove for the front of the vehicle and the door on the driver's side, knowing only that she had to escape. She was vaguely aware that Rusty had swung around and thrown his body between her and the gunman, pushing her forward.

She scrambled over the seat and swung open the driver's door. The next second she was plowing into another dark-suited gunman, his bulk terminating any hope of flight. She winced and stifled a yelp as he grabbed her wrist, swallowing it up in his beefy hand.

Twisting it, the gunman shoved her back inside. Dakota rammed her knee on the seat as she stumbled down beside Rusty. He caught her to keep her from falling.

"Hey, look, buddy, I don't know who you are, but we're supposed to be here." Rusty began to reach for the clipboard on the floor with its doctored work orders that Megan had e-mailed him. He pulled his hand back just in time. The giant in the black suit at the rear door shot a hole through the board, and most likely, through the floor of the vehicle, as well.

"You reach for one more thing, punk, and it's the last thing you'll ever reach for." The gunman waved the recently fired gun at them. "Now get out of the damn truck."

Dakota was too frustrated and too angry to be afraid. There was fury in her eyes as she pulled back from the beefy hand that was about to drag her out of the vehicle.

"I can walk on my own," she spat.

The man laughed. The sound was far from friendly. It sent shivers down her spine. "You must have been one handful for Vincent Junior."

She resented the familiarity in the man's voice, resented his saying anything about the man who had touched her life. "You're not fit to say his name."

"Dakota, keep your mouth shut if you want to keep on breathing long enough to see your son," Rusty told her sharply.

She looked at Rusty in surprise.

"I'd listen to the man if I were you. He's making sense," the man who'd fired at the clipboard said, stepping back to allow them both to leave the truck.

Her immediate reaction was to shout at Rusty that he should keep his own mouth shut, but she knew he was right. He was just trying to keep the situation as defused as possible. Going off like a Roman candle wasn't going to help anyone, least of all Vinny.

It took all of her willpower, but she pressed her lips together and raised her arms the way the other gunman ordered. She got out of the truck, followed closely by Rusty. The second henchman brought up the rear.

"This way," the first man said. "But then, you already know that, don't you, hot stuff?"

Too bad looks couldn't kill, Dakota thought. The one Andreini gave the man would have more than done the trick.

Guns at their backs, Dakota and Rusty were herded down the hill like wayward cattle.

"Not exactly the way I pictured this," she hissed to Rusty.

"Give it time," he responded under his breath, "it's early."

"Hey, you two," the first gunman warned, "shut up."

"We're shutting," Rusty assured him amiably.

Dakota sneered. "My hero."

"Eventually," was all Rusty said in reply.

She should live so long, Dakota thought angrily.

A tall, thin man was waiting inside the mansion to open the door and let them in. It was obvious to Rusty that the henchman with the happy trigger finger had called ahead. Rusty recognized the thin man from the day before, when he'd brought in the groceries.

"I see they promoted you to the front," Rusty commented mildly as he passed him. "You were guarding the rear door yesterday, weren't you?"

The man scowled, his dark, bushy eyebrows forming a single, hairy line over his intense blue eyes.

"Knew you were a phony. No more deliveries to make?" the man jeered as he stuck his face into Rusty's. Closing the door, he gave Rusty a shove that propelled him into the foyer. "Get moving."

Dakota entered first. A feeling of unwanted familiarity washed over her. The last time she'd been in this house, in this living room, she'd been nine months pregnant, listening to Vincent's father outline the rest of her usefulness to him. She'd been nothing more than a vessel to him. Less. He'd made that abundantly clear with each word he'd uttered, every look he'd slanted at her.

He was here, waiting for them.

Her eyes filled with hate as she looked at Del Greco, a small, meticulously groomed man presiding over his empire sitting on a sofa that cost more than most people's houses.

He'd made a point of telling her that. He had thought it would help to intimidate her, to give him the upper hand. He'd gone on at length about all the benefits that would be the baby's once he was born.

Benefits someone like her couldn't hope to give a child. As he'd droned on, all she could think of was that Vincent had hated growing up in this cold mausoleum.

When Del Greco'd concluded, contempt in his eyes as he looked at her, she'd wanted nothing more than to spit in his face. But she'd played it safe for the sake of her unborn child and pretended to want a little time to think things through.

Del Greco had thought she was angling for more money and let her go, confident that she would see things his way. There was no other way, no other options open to a woman like her.

Aristocratic fingers folded in front of him, Del Greco regarded the woman who had borne his grandson. He didn't bother attempting to mask his contempt. He knew that his mistake had been in thinking that she was too afraid of him and too smart to run, so he had let her return to her small apartment to arrive at the right decision, the decision he'd felt confident she would make.

He'd come within an inch of shooting the soldier who had brought him the news that she had vanished. Vincent Del Greco did not take disappointment well.

His glare sliced her apart. "You should have taken the money I offered you." The laugh that followed was short. "But then, Vincent was always hooking up with stupid bimbos. He was weak that way."

Dakota let the insult go. She knew Del Greco was merely trying to get at her. But the stakes were far beyond petty things such as name-calling. She couldn't care less what Vincent Del Greco thought of her. All she wanted was her son.

She took a step toward him. "Where is he, you bastard? Where's my son?"

She heard the click of a weapon and felt rather than saw it being pointed at her by Del Greco's solider. Rusty shifted beside her, as if to cover her with the only thing he had at his disposal, his own body. Dakota ignored the reaction the selfless act generated within her.

Like a magnanimous emperor, Del Greco waved back his henchman, his small, steely eyes boring hot holes into Dakota.

"What the hell are you talking about?" he demanded. "And where's my grandson while you're out, keeping this guy's sheets warm?"

The ploy nearly pushed her over the edge. It took everything she had to not lunge at the man, henchmen or no henchmen.

"You should know, you took him. Don't play dumb with me, old man, it doesn't suit you. Now, give Vinny back to me, or I swear—"

Del Greco cut her off. "You're in no position to swear. Pray, maybe, if anyone up there will hear the prayers of a two-bit whore like you." The look on Del Greco's face clearly indicated that he felt her prayers would be a waste of time and breath. He rose to his feet. Barely containing his rage, his small body shook. Del Greco grabbed her by the throat, tilting her head upward. "Now, what are you talking about?"

He was squeezing so hard, she could hardly breathe and tears of pain rose in her eyes.

"Let her go," Rusty ordered. Any move to help was cut short by the barrel of the gun shoved into his side.

"Shut up, tough guy, your turn'll come." Del Greco's eyes fairly glittered as he focused them on Dakota, never slackening his hold on her throat. "Now, talk."

"My son," Dakota rasped, the words crawling up the small space he had left her for air. "I want my son. You had your men take him and I want him back."

For a split second, Rusty detected bewilderment in the gray-blue eyes before it was replaced by contempt and hatred.

"You lost him?" Del Greco shouted, pushing her back so hard she stumbled and would have fallen if Rusty hadn't caught her.

"You took him," she insisted, shaking Rusty off as she continued to glare at Del Greco. "Where is he?"

Disbelief warred with rage. "You stupid bitch. You lost my grandson?"

Shaken, Dakota was torn. Was this an act or wasn't it? The man was a born liar, smooth and charming one minute, ruthless and cold-blooded the next. She didn't know what to believe.

"If you didn't take him, who did?" Rusty wanted to know.

Del Greco looked at him sharply. "Who the hell are you?"

"The man I hired to get my son back," Dakota retorted hotly.

The uneasy feeling that they had plunged into a hornet's nest for no reason was slowly taking hold in the pit of her stomach. If Del Greco was telling the truth, if he didn't have Vinny, who did? There'd been no ransom note, no call. Why hadn't they contacted her? She'd checked the messages on her answering machine via the remote feature every chance she got. There had been no demands for ransom, no calls that could be followed up at all.

Where was Vinny? Who had him?

Scorn made Del Greco's face almost skeletal in appearance. "Well, if he led you here, you wasted your money." He looked up angrily as one of his men entered the room. "Get out of here, Johnny. This is a private matter."

But the tall man moved toward him, not away. "Mr. Del Greco, I think you'll want to see this," Johnny said softly, indicating the manila envelope he was holding.

Like a messenger afraid of being killed because of the message, he placed the opened envelope in Del Greco's hands and then backed away.

Del Greco looked at the envelope in silence, as if he already knew what would be inside. A sixth sense, the instinct that had gotten him to the seat of power he occupied today and had kept him alive, told him what he would find within the envelope. So did the expression on the face of the man who had brought the envelope to him. His men were under orders to quickly open all suspicious-looking mail addressed to him.

This appeared to have been left rather than mailed.

"Mr. Del Greco, if you want, I could—" the capo at his side began. Del Greco waved him into silence, his eyes never leaving the offending envelope.

Hardly breathing, Dakota watched as Del Greco slipped his long, narrow fingers into the padded envelope. As much as she didn't want to, she believed the aging crime boss. He hadn't taken Vinny. The pallor of the man's complexion exonerated him.

Barely suppressing his anguish, Del Greco pulled out a small plastic bag with a dark lock of hair inside it. Dakota bit back a cry of recognition and despair. There was no question in her mind.

"That's Vinny's hair."

For a second the man by whose authority they were being held prisoner looked twice as old as his sixty-three years. Clutching the plastic bag to him as if it were precious, he unfolded the letter. There was very little writing on it.

"It's Stavos." Rage vibrated in his throat. Starting out as an annoyance five years ago, Stavos and his organization had steadily grown, encroaching on his territory. Now he wanted it all. "He says if we don't back off from the casinos, he'll kill Vinny."

The next moment the broken, vulnerable look was gone as if it had never existed. Suddenly he was Vin-

cent Del Greco, the head of a proud family, the chief
of a multilayered crime organization.

"He wants to negotiate. Negotiate for my grandson!" Viciousness erupted. "I'll give him negotiate."
He looked at his first-in-command. "Get the boys together, we have some 'talking' to do."

The second man exchanged looks with Johnny before addressing his question to Del Greco. "What do
you want me to do with these two?"

Del Greco paused to look at Dakota and Rusty. He
acted as if he'd forgotten they were even there and,
now that he remembered, felt they weren't worth a
microsecond of his time.

"Take them out into the desert and get rid of them.
I don't care how you do it, just do it."

"You can't go and confront this Stavos," Dakota
cried even as she and Rusty were being taken from
the room. "He'll kill Vinny."

Her warning had no effect on Del Greco. "He's
too smart to do that. He knows if he does, it's his
death warrant."

"And what are you, invulnerable?" she demanded
sarcastically. "Immortal?"

He stopped just long enough to give her a triumphant smirk.

"Damn straight I am, cookie." The smile faded
from his mouth, to be replaced by one of pure ma-
levolence. "Now get them the hell out of here before
I do the job myself right here." Del Greco looked
down at the white rug beneath his feet, the rug he had
replaced every year in his desire to keep the outward

signs of purity close at hand. "Rug's due to be replaced anyway."

"Your grandson might get killed in the crossfire," Rusty pointed out.

Nearly out of range, Del Greco stopped, taken by the calm cadence in the voice of a man who had perhaps only an hour to live, perhaps less.

"You let me worry about my grandson, hired gun." The evil smile was back. "I'd say you've got bigger concerns of your own right now." His eyes shifted to the man he was entrusting with the assignment. "Take Johnny with you. And a shovel. I don't want a trace left, understand?"

"Sure thing, Mr. Del Greco," the henchman said, bobbing his head in respect for both the man and the position he held. He aimed his weapon at Dakota. "You heard the man, move."

Rusty saw the expression on Dakota's face. An alarm went off in his head. She was going to do something, something stupid that would most likely get her killed. They had to wait until the odds were not six to two against them. He caught her eye and shook his head slowly. To his relief, though there was contempt in her eyes, she angrily acquiesced.

It bought him some time to think.

Chapter 14

"You really don't want to do this."

Stuffed beside Dakota in the back seat of a compact car, his hands tied behind his back, Rusty addressed the words to the man who had been ordered to terminate them. He purposely avoided looking at the gun the man, Johnny, was holding.

Johnny, obviously uncomfortable, was sitting twisted around in the front passenger seat. He appeared in no mood for any kind of a conversation.

"Shut up," the burly man ordered.

"Better think about it," Rusty cautioned, his voice mild, in direct contrast to the thoughts racing through his head.

There had to be a way out. They were heading into the heart of the desert. Only Redhawk knew where they had initially been, but it was unrealistic to think that they could rely on him for any kind of help. The detective had no way of knowing they were in trouble.

He'd been in better situations. "Killing us is really going to look bad on Santa's naughty list. You'll be finding coal in your stocking until you die."

Johnny looked exactly one step away from pistol-whipping him into silence. "I said *shut up*." Turning, he looked impatiently at the driver. "Pick a place, you moron. My back's killing me."

The driver looked at him resentfully. "Mr. Del Greco said to make it desolate."

"It's the desert," Johnny snapped angrily. "It's all desolate."

"Okay." The driver abruptly stopped the car and pulled up the emergency hand brake.

Johnny nodded his approval. A malevolent smile began to form on his thick lips. "This is it, folks. Last stop. And I mean last stop."

Getting out first, he opened the back door and pulled Rusty out roughly. He reached for Dakota next.

She shrank back from him, not wanting to endure his touch. But there was nowhere to go. He grabbed her by the arm and yanked her out.

Dakota recovered herself quickly. "You really like your work, don't you?"

Surprised at her tone, Rusty looked at her. Her voice was oddly devoid of contempt, the way he'd expected. She'd certainly made no effort to hide her feelings from Del Greco earlier.

Dakota slanted a look back to the car. The driver,

she noted, remained where he was, apparently content to turn what was about to happen into a spectator sport for his personal amusement.

She felt her blood run cold and purposely ignored it. There wasn't time to feel anything.

"Yeah." Malice highlighted the smile on his moon face, forming deep ruts. "I do."

Moving ever so slightly to the side, forcing Johnny to turn his back to the vehicle, she swept her eyes over him with an unmistakable invitation. When she spoke again, her voice was soft, seductive. "Bet I could get you to like something else more."

Because there was no hurry and no way for the two they'd brought out here in the middle of nowhere to avoid their fates, she knew Del Greco's executioner would see no harm in listening to what she had to say. No harm in perhaps enjoying himself before he did what was expected of him.

There was no doubt in his mind about the ultimate outcome here today. No matter what the luscious, statuesque blonde came up with, how she intended to bargain for her life, he was going to terminate both of them just as he'd been told to do. Del Greco was not a man to cross.

But that didn't mean he couldn't get himself a little early Christmas cheer.

He ran fat, sausage-like fingers through her hair. "What'd you have in mind, honey?"

It took everything she had not to shiver in revulsion. She indicated the ropes that held her hands fast behind her back. "You know, I do a lot better with my hands free."

"Yeah, I bet." His laugh was nothing short of evil. "But for what I've got in mind, honey, you won't be needing your hands." He looked at her pointedly, already anticipating the rush he was going to feel. His palms grew sweaty. "And who knows, if you're nice to me, maybe I'll be nice to you."

She looked at him in wide-eyed innocence. "You'll let us go?"

Johnny pretended to consider the matter, then nodded. "You," he lied. "Maybe."

She knew it would look too suspicious if she leaped at that. Dakota took a beat. "No, it has to be him, too."

It cost Johnny nothing to lie. And it beat the hell out of arguing. He wanted to get on with it, to see just how far she would go to barter for her life.

"We'll see." His eyes all but disappeared as he smiled in anticipation. "Now, let's see what you can do for me."

"Right here?" she asked, her eyes wide. "In front of everyone?"

Like that would bother him, Johnny thought, laughing. "Sure, I'm not shy."

Dakota slowly licked her lips, watching the man's reaction. Good, she had him. "All right, then, neither am I."

With slow, deliberate movements, she came toward him, a living, breathing portrait of seduction. There was perspiration forming on his brow where his hair had receded. Dakota wet her lips again, then tilted her head as if to kiss the gunman.

The next moment she brought her knee up as hard as she could.

With a horrified squeal of pain, the burly man went down, dropping his weapon as he clutched at the source of his agony. Afraid that he would be up on his feet as soon as he managed his pain, she brought her heel down on top of his clutching hands for good measure.

He screamed. There was no breath left with which to curse her.

"What the hell are you doing?" the driver yelled, leaping out of the car.

As the driver cleared the vehicle, Rusty head-butted him, sending him crashing to the ground. They had no time to lose. Rusty turned to Dakota and saw that, though tied, her hands were now out in front of her rather than behind her. And her fingers were wrapped around the gun of the man writhing in pain on the ground beside her.

He nodded at her hands. "How did you manage that?"

She spared him a self-satisfied smile. "I'm agile, remember?"

Fragments of last night replayed themselves swiftly through his head. That was the word for it, all right. "Yeah, I forgot about that."

Gun firmly between her hands, Dakota pointed the weapon at the driver who was beginning to come around. He moaned as he clutched his head.

"You, untie him." She raised the nuzzle so that it was pointed at his head. There was no mistaking her intent. "Now."

Cursing at her and at his disabled partner still howling his pain, the driver did as he was told.

With his hands freed, Rusty reached for the weapon in hers. "Thanks, that was quick thinking."

Watching the driver for any sudden moves, Dakota surrendered the gun to Rusty. He took it like a man comfortable with a weapon in his hands. "I thought you didn't believe in guns."

"Doesn't mean I don't know how to use one." He waved the weapon at the driver, motioning him over. "Free her," he ordered. He spared a glance at the man on the ground. Despite everything, he could still empathize with his pain, feeling it clear down to his own marrow. Dakota Armstrong, he decided, was a force to be reckoned with. "How hard did you kick him?"

"Hard enough," was all she said.

Free, she was careful to step back from the driver in case he wanted to try anything. She wasn't about to become an unwitting hostage.

Of like mind, Rusty waved the driver away from her as Dakota rubbed her wrists to get the circulation back. "Okay, now tie him up." He indicated the gunman on the ground.

Eyes moving from one face to the other, the driver began to sweat profusely. "Look, I wasn't going to kill you. He was." He pointed at Johnny, his voice rising in panic. "I'm just a driver."

Rusty's face remained impassive. "Right, we're all just following orders. Now follow mine." His tone was low and eerily menacing. "Tie him up."

The driver did as he was told, his hands shaking as he made the knots. Dakota leaned over to check them, careful to stay clear of his hands. The man on the ground cursed her weakly.

Rusty got the rest of the rope out of the trunk and tossed it to Dakota. "Tie up the driver," he told her.

"Nothing would give me more pleasure." With swift movements, she wove the rope around the man's hands, then his feet, leaving him hog-tied beside his partner. "Doesn't feel so good when the shoe's on the other foot, does it?" she said to him.

Gun still at the ready, Rusty watched her. The woman was magnificent. It wasn't a new thought for him. "You don't panic under fire, do you?"

"If I did, we'd both be dead." Satisfied that the ropes were secure, she stepped back. "Those knots should hold well," she told him. "They're not getting free any time soon."

Rusty nodded, already walking to the car. "Okay, let's get out of here."

"What about us?" the driver cried after them. "You can't just leave us here."

Rusty got in on the driver's side. His eyes showed no emotion. "Watch me."

"We'll die out here," the driver sputtered, thrashing around like a newly caught fish.

"That's the main idea," was all Rusty said before starting up the car and driving away.

Strapping on her seat belt, Dakota twisted around to watch as the two figures on the ground behind her grew smaller, merging with the horizon. There was nothing to see except occasional brush for miles around. It was winter, but it was still fairly warm during the daytime. When night fell, so did the temperature. Not to mention that there were coyotes in the area. The two henchmen's chances of surviving were slim to none.

Dakota shifted back around to face forward. She didn't want Johnny and the driver's deaths on her conscience, even though they'd already proven that hers wouldn't have affected either one of theirs. She studied Rusty's profile for a moment, her pulse still racing from their narrow escape.

This wasn't like him, she thought. "Are you really going to leave them there?"

He turned toward her ever so slightly, not sure if it was idle curiosity or concern he heard in her voice. "Would it bother you?"

She pressed her lips together, examining her conscience. "It shouldn't, but yeah, it would."

That she had compassion for her would-be executioners in the midst of the turmoil she was enduring heartened him. Compassion was one of the qualities he most admired and required in those closest to him.

He nodded, as if to approve of her answer. "I'll call Gray as soon as my phone gets into network range," he promised. It was what he'd planned to do anyway.

Dakota tried to sit back and relax, but couldn't. She was far too worried. "Now what?"

Until they could reach Gray, they had only one course open to them. To follow Del Greco. "Have you any idea where Enrique Stavos lives?"

Dakota laughed shortly. The crime head's residence was no secret. "Everyone does. It's the showiest place in Nevada, bar none. And considering this is Las Vegas, that's saying a lot."

"Good, you can give me directions while I drive." He set his mouth grimly, not wanting to allow his thoughts to get too far ahead of him. "Let's hope we get there before all hell breaks loose."

She seconded that thought silently.

With Dakota's directions to guide him, Rusty drove to Enrique Stavos's estate, a desert palace that would have made a sultan drool.

With the sun fully up, the ostentatiousness of the forty-room residence was hard to miss even at a distance. As Rusty made it out, he grimaced. The edifice was a monument to bad taste. It was surrounded by a fifteen-foot, black-iron fence. At the front, ten-foot-tall, carved white-marble horses reared on their hind legs, forever frozen in mid-motion on either side of the gate.

Way too loud for his tastes, Rusty thought. "Thinks big, doesn't he?"

"Word has it, he always has." Once she'd found out about Vincent's background, he'd filled her in on everyone. He'd said that he wanted her to know what he was leaving behind to be with her. Wanting to be larger than life in his own way, Vincent had left nothing out. It was then that he'd given her the diary.

"Stavos makes no secret of his ambition. He wants to own a piece of everything that exists in Las Vegas." Hence the casino war. Her mouth hardened as she clenched her fists on either side of her. "And he's using my son to get what he wants."

"Not for long," Rusty promised her.

He took the hill down to the gates quickly, driving as if the very engine was on fire and he had only moments to get to where he was going before it exploded. He'd called Graham Redhawk the moment he'd been able to get a transmitting signal, only to learn that Gray was unavailable.

Belatedly, Rusty remembered that the man's wife had gone into labor yesterday. Gray was probably still at the hospital or glorying in the joys of fatherhood. Leaving an abbreviated message to patch through to him at the first opportunity, Rusty had made a beeline for the Stavos estate.

For the time being, they were on their own.

Rusty knew that it would have been more prudent to wait for help to arrive, but prudent might lose them the boy and that was what this was all about, getting the boy back.

Before they could manage to reach the front gates, Rusty saw them begin to open. A black limousine raced through before the gates were fully retracted.

Someone was in one hell of a hurry to get away, he thought.

In the distance, they heard gunfire.

"He's in there," Dakota cried suddenly, grabbing hold of Rusty's arm, and pointing at the limousine.

He squinted as a cloud of dust formed in the vehicle's wake. "Mother's instincts?"

"Perfect vision," she corrected. He squinted harder. And made out a piece of red flannel material flapping cheerfully out of one window. "That's Vinny's blanket. They took him in it. He won't go anywhere without it." She would have known it anywhere.

Making a turn so sharp that their car was nearly balanced on two wheels, Rusty spun the car around and tore after the limousine in hot pursuit.

"Hang on," he warned her, stepping down hard on the accelerator, "this is going to get bumpy."

"No kidding." Dakota grabbed the overhead strap and did as he said. He was taking twists and turns as if he were a fifteen-year veteran of the race-car circuit. "Where did you learn how to drive like this?"

A fond smile slipped over his lips. "Drag races in high school." He spared her a single glance before turning his eyes back to the road. Keeping the vehicle from crashing required his complete attention. "I'm not as mild-mannered as I seem."

"You already proved that," Dakota murmured under her breath.

But he'd heard her. And knew she was talking about last night.

Good, she hadn't managed to wipe it from her mind

the way she'd tried to make him believe. He had a foundation. Rusty figured it was all he needed.

He thought he heard the sound of gunfire behind him again, but he couldn't be sure. It might just have been a car backfiring. In any case, he had no time to speculate. The limousine ahead of him was capable of remarkable speed, given its size. The man behind the wheel was obviously a pro.

But, Rusty silently vowed, he'd met his match today.

Several miles later the road divided into what looked to be two neat parallel lines. Making a decision, Rusty pushed down on the accelerator as far as it would go. He needed to get ahead of the vehicle.

Dakota looked at the speedometer. The needle was flirting outrageously with the one hundred mark. She could hear the car whining and rattling in protest. But they were passing the limousine.

"What are you doing?" she demanded. Had he lost his mind? She pulled on his arm to get his attention. "The limousine's back there."

"I know." He glanced at her fleetingly. "We have to get in front of them. I've got a plan."

She let go of his arm and tried not to worry. "Finally."

"Finally?" He didn't know if she was being serious or just wry. "I thought we were doing pretty well up to now."

"'Pretty well' isn't good enough." Still hanging on to the strap, Dakota was rigid with tension as she strained to see the other car. "I still don't have my son."

"But you will," he promised. "You will."

So he kept saying. So she kept praying. "So what's this plan of yours?"

"To get ahead of him," he repeated.

He glanced at the dials on the dashboard, hoping the car wouldn't overheat or give out before he got to where he was going. If he were driving his own car, he'd be feeling a lot more confident about its capabilities. He'd tinkered with it and tuned it until it handled like a fine stallion. He was driving blindly with this car and could only pray it would hold out long enough to get the job done.

Judging that he was far enough ahead of the limousine, Rusty turned the wheel sharply and drove over the brush to reach the first road. The passage was jarring. They only had a couple of minutes at most before the limousine reached them.

Once there, he drove a little farther until he came to a spot that was right for his plan. "This is it," he announced, braking abruptly.

The car shuddered and shook, very nearly spinning out of control before it finally halted. He angled it sideways so that there would be no way for the other vehicle to pass them.

"All right," he reached to the left of the steering column and pulled the lever he found there. "I'm going to pop the hood. I want you to get out of the car and pretend to be stranded." He got out himself. "Look your damn sexiest." Looking at her, he took back his instruction. "Never mind, you're already doing that."

She flushed at the compliment, vainly trying to shake it off. She had no business savoring compliments when her child was still in jeopardy.

Hands on her shoulders, he kissed her quickly. "For luck." And then he hurried away.

Stunned, she stared after Rusty. "Where are you going?"

"I won't be far," was all he had time to tell her. The limousine was approaching in the distance. He had to find a place to hide before the driver saw him.

"God, I hope you know what you're doing," she murmured under her breath. Especially since he had taken the gun with him.

Swallowing, she saw the limousine driving straight for her. Dakota raised her arms and began waving at the driver in abject distress.

"Wait, please," she called, doing her best imitation of Marilyn Monroe. "I need help."

Because there was no way around her, the limousine stopped several feet away. The driver got out, cursing loudly.

"What the hell do you think you're doing?" he demanded. "Get your car out of the road, lady, before I ram it out of the way."

"That's just it. I can't." She looked accusingly over her shoulder at the vehicle. "It won't go. Not another inch."

The driver scowled darkly, looking at the obstacle.

He obviously had no time for delays. "It will if I plow my car through it."

Dakota grabbed his arm, her eyes wide in supplication. "But you can't do that. How will I get into Vegas? I'll miss my afternoon show. The director said he'd fire me if I was late again."

Her effort hadn't failed her. For the first time, the attributes of the woman making her plea began to register on Stavos's chauffeur. She shuddered inwardly as a leer formed on his lips as he gave her the once-over. "You're welcome to ride with us, honey. You can even sit in the front with me. If you promise to be really grateful."

To liken the man to a gorilla would have been insulting to gorillas everywhere, she thought. Dakota forced a smile to her lips.

"Oh, I will," she breathed, hanging on to his arm and deliberately keeping his back to the limousine. "I'll be ever so grateful to you."

With the driver occupied, Rusty took his chance. He hurried out of the brush where he'd managed to hide. Crouching, with time ticking away, he yanked open the rear door, his weapon trained at whoever was next to the window.

The man inside looked surprised, but recovered instantly. He lunged for Rusty's weapon. As they grappled for control, the gun discharged.

Dakota screamed, afraid to think past the sound. Whirling around to see what was going on, the driver cursed, then began running toward the car. Frantic, knowing she had to do something to keep him away from Rusty, Dakota picked up a rock, aimed and then hurled it at the back of his head. She hit her mark and he went down.

Running past his prone body, she was in time to see Rusty order the other man away from the vehicle. He stumbled out, his hands raised. He left the door open.

Inside, cowering on the black leather seat, clutching his blanket and vainly trying to fade into the upholstery, was her son.

Dakota thought her heart would break from the sight.

"Oh, baby, it's all right. Mommy's here. She's here." Tears threatened to choke her as she slid into the car beside her son.

"Mommy?" The little boy said her name as if he thought he was dreaming. He blinked and she was still there. With a cry of joy, he flung himself into her arms. "No more bad men," he pleaded with her. "No more bad men."

"No more bad men," she echoed, hugging him to her, stroking his silky hair. She pressed a kiss to the top of his head, unable to believe that he was finally safe again. "I promise, sweetie."

Quickly she got out of the car, still holding her son in her arms. He was wrapped around her like a monkey, still holding on to his precious blanket. She didn't want to frighten Vinny, but the sooner they got away from here, the better.

"I've got him, let's go," she said to Rusty, hurrying to their car.

When he didn't follow her, she turned around to urge him on again.

It was then she saw the blood splattered on his shoulder.

Chapter 15

More adrenaline poured into her bloodstream.

Worried, Dakota touched Rusty's shoulder lightly. Her fingers felt sticky. She stared at them in horror.

Words came to her after the fact. "Omigod, Andreini, you're hurt."

Wiping the blood from her fingers onto her jeans, she held her son close to her as she scanned Rusty's torso for more wounds. There appeared to be only one. The bullet had not gone through. It was still lodged within him.

He winced when she touched him and cursed inwardly. He wasn't supposed to show pain. Rusty struggled to keep the fog circling his brain at bay.

"Tell me something I don't know." It felt as if his shoulder were on fire. Sweat popped out on his brow as he fought against the fierce pain. "Don't worry, it's a flesh wound."

As if she didn't know the difference. Who did he think he was, John Wayne? "That's an awful lot of blood for a flesh wound."

"Yeah, well, I don't believe in doing things in half measures." His head was spinning badly and his legs were beginning to feel rubbery. "Dakota, how good are you with a gun?"

Something was terribly wrong if he was surrendering the gun. She tried to not let her mounting panic break through. "I can blow an apple off a gopher's head at thirty paces."

"I had a feeling." Carefully, keeping his eyes on the other man, Rusty transferred the weapon to Dakota. It was beginning to feel heavier than he knew it should. He needed to sit someplace before he fell over. "We're fresh out of apples, but see what you can do with this weasel. I'm going to try to raise Gray again."

Knees buckling, Rusty sank down onto the passenger seat of the limo that had so recently held Vinny and his captor. Rusty fumbled for his cell phone, trying to remember which pocket he'd put it in.

He was making her really worried. "You don't look so good, Rusty."

With effort, he focused on her. The woman was magnificent. Standing there, one arm wrapped around her son, the other extended, holding a gun trained on the henchman, she looked like the modern equivalent of a pioneer woman protecting her family. He figured she was worried, otherwise she wouldn't have called him by his first name. Even in his confused state, he found the thought comforting.

"I don't feel too well," he replied. The driver was beginning to stir. Rusty knew that he should check the man for a weapon, but his head was spinning badly now and he really didn't trust his legs to make the short trip. "Dakota, he might have—"

"A gun," she concluded. "Right. Way ahead of you." She placed her son within the limousine. He looked up at her with vivid, quizzical eyes. She kissed the top of his head. "Vinny, you stay with the nice man."

Vinny looked at Rusty and offered him a shy smile. "Nice man," he echoed.

"Yes, baby, very nice man," she assured him, then hurried to the prone body sprawled out on the ground. She needed to frisk him before he came to.

Moving swiftly, she checked the usual places for a concealed weapon and was successful on her fourth attempt. She pulled the gun free of its holster and tucked it into her own waistband.

Watching her, Rusty thought of every fantasy he'd ever had as a teenager about strong, sexy women. "You do that like a pro," he managed to say.

"You learn a few things living on the wrong side of Las Vegas," she told him as she started crossing toward the limousine again.

"Get down!" Rusty yelled, bolting up from his seat just as she reached him.

The next moment she felt him push her roughly to

the ground. Above her head a single round of gunfire being exchanged resounded, throbbing in her ears. She could have swore she'd felt a bullet whiz by her head as she'd gone down.

Scrambling to her feet, it took her a second to pull everything into focus. The man behind her had had another gun on him, a snubnose that had fit into the front of his pants. She'd checked his legs for a second weapon, but missed that one because he'd been lying on his stomach.

She watched the pool of blood spread on the ground. The driver was dead.

His partner stood rooted to the spot, his hands raised high over his head. She was barely conscious of him, leaving that to Rusty. Hurrying to her son, Dakota picked him up and held him against her. He was whimpering again. She silently swore to spend the rest of her life making this up to him.

Turning, she looked at Rusty. He was even paler now than he had been a moment ago.

Gratitude shone in her eyes. "You certainly do earn your pay."

"I try," he murmured.

"We can tie him up." She nodded at the other man. "I want to take a look at that shoulder." The blood was soaking into his jacket at an alarming rate.

But he shook his head. He began pressing the cell phone keypad again. "Not until after I get through to Gray."

She was about to tell him that she didn't think he could wait. She'd taken some nursing courses in hopes of eventually getting a degree and knew an ugly wound when she saw one, even when it was partially hidden by a jacket. But the sound of sirens in the distance disrupted any tug-of-war of wills that was about to happen.

"I'd say you don't have to bother." She nodded toward the direction of the sirens. Beautiful music to her ears. "Sounds like help is on the way."

Within moments Detective Graham Redhawk was hurrying out of his pink pride and joy to join them. It took him less time than that to assess the situation.

He shook his head, pushing back his black Stetson. "I was coming to the rescue, but it looks like you two don't need my help. You seem to have things pretty well in hand." His eyes crinkled as he smiled at the little boy in Dakota's arms. "I take it that this is the brave soldier you were looking for."

Vinny responded to Gray's voice and the approval in it. He smiled shyly, then hid his head, winding his arms more tightly around Dakota's neck.

Dakota thought her heart was going to burst. "This is him," Dakota verified with pride.

There were three squad cars in all, counting Gray's. The rest had been deployed to the Stavos estate and had remained there. "Looks like I get to clean up."

"How did you know we were here?" Dakota wanted to know.

"They patched his message through to me at the hospital. I figured you probably needed me more than Caitlin did. My wife's resting right now. It was a long labor.'' And she had come through like a trouper, he thought. She always did.

"What did you have?" Rusty asked weakly.

"Girl. Just like her big brother ordered," Gray added. "I followed you out here after one of the men inside the estate 'volunteered' that two of Stavos's men were headed for the airport with the boy. I figured you'd be right behind them." Gray nodded in the direction from which they'd come. "You left quite a mess back there."

"It wasn't our doing," Rusty assured him. That had undoubtedly been the result of the confrontation between the warring organizations. Drained now that Dakota was safe, Rusty sank down again in the car. "The limousine was just leaving when we arrived. We went right after it."

Gray eyed the wound. He'd seen a lot worse, but it was far from good. "What happened to you?"

"Cut myself shaving," Rusty quipped, though it cost him.

Gray laughed under his breath. "Yeah, I hear you hairy Caucasians spend a lot of money on razors." Placing a hand under Rusty's arm, he helped him slowly to his feet. "C'mon, let's get you in the car. I'll take you to the nearest hospital. You and Dakota can fill me in on your 'nonparticipation' on the way over."

Rusty was leaning on the man more than he was happy about, but he knew that if he tried to be stubborn about it, he wasn't going to make it to the vehicle under his own power. He'd used up all of his available strength pushing Dakota out of the way.

"Aren't you afraid I'll get blood on your car?"

Gray grinned as he brought Rusty over to one of the two black-and-whites. "That's why we're using a squad car." He lowered Rusty into the back seat as gently as if he were setting down his new baby daughter. "By the way—" he turned to look at Dakota "—I thought you might want to know, Del Greco's dead."

She froze, stunned. Afraid to believe her own ears. "What?"

He nodded. "Dead. We identified his body when we arrived." He opened the opposite door for her and Vinny. "It's too soon to tell, but it looks like the bullet might have come from one of his own men's guns. My guess it was someone looking to change organizations and eager to get on the good side of Stavos." He closed the door behind Dakota and her son, then rounded the hood to get in behind the wheel. "In any case, it's going to take us a while to sort things out."

Gray shook his head, starting the car. "Times like this, I wish I had gone into tribal medicine." He glanced over his shoulder at his passengers. "No pension plan, but you sure can't beat the hours."

Dead. Vincent Del Greco was dead. The man who had haunted her every waking and sleeping moment was dead.

She breathed a sigh of relief.

As if reading her mind, Rusty placed his hand over hers and offered her a weak smile.

She was drained, completely, utterly drained. In the background, the TV she'd left on was into the second hour of *It's a Wonderful Life* but she barely heard it.

Sinking down onto the sofa, she felt almost numb. She told herself to snap out of it and to count her blessings. After all, they really were bountiful. She had Vinny back, something she would always be eternally grateful for, and she didn't have to run anymore. Del Greco, the only one who truly wanted to take her son, was dead. He couldn't hurt her or Vinny anymore.

To insure that his organization would be dismantled, she'd taken Vincent's diary and mailed it anonymously to the Nevada D.A.'s office after first wiping it clean of her own fingerprints as well as Rusty's. She'd only touched the thick volume once with her bare hands, using gloves to turn the pages once she realized what the book contained. She hoped it would help the D.A. make an ironclad case against everyone left alive in Del Greco's crime syndicate.

She was free. Really free.

So why didn't she feel that way? Why was there this awful heavy feeling pressing down on her chest, making her feel disoriented? Why wouldn't it go away?

Restless, she got up just as George Bailey encountered Clarence, his second-class angel. Maybe she felt like this because she knew she would never see Rusty again.

Maybe? It was a sure thing. She'd already made up her mind that she was moving away as soon as she found another apartment. One more move. Hopefully, the last one she would have to make for a long, long time.

Still running, aren't you? she mocked herself.

But what else could she do? At the hospital where Gray had taken them, she'd confided in Rusty in a moment of weakness, probably because of all the blood that he had lost, and said that she was beginning to realize that some people could actually be trusted.

He'd taken that small opening to mean that she was talking about him and proposed.

Proposed.

Of all the stupid, misguided things to do. He hadn't picked up on her cue when she'd suddenly fallen silent, and he had continued. He'd told her that he wanted to be around to take care of her. She'd snapped at him then and informed him that she didn't need taking care of, that she was fine by herself and that she certainly didn't need anyone proposing to her.

And he hadn't said anything. Not a word. Just nodded and walked away.

Maybe the whole thing had been a joke on his part. Otherwise, wouldn't he have pressed? Wouldn't he have tried to convince her to say yes? Wouldn't he have tried to talk her out of this raw fear that had

seized her heart, the fear that if she let her heart loose,
it was going to be forever lost, forever useless to her?

She'd been battered around emotionally for most
of her life; she needed some assurances that that
wasn't going to happen again.

He was a detective, damn him, why couldn't he
detect her fear and talk her out of it?

She blinked. Behind her, on the TV set, people
were sharing the holidays with a Christmas beer in
one of the endlessly cheerful commercials littering the
airwaves. She could feel her eyes smarting.

Oh, no, she wasn't going to cry. She couldn't. She
refused. She had Vinny; she had a new life; now she
could finally move on. Everything was great. Just
great.

She just had to remember that.

She looked at the set just as another commercial
came on with carolers singing in front of a huge tree.
Dakota looked at the empty spot she'd cleared away
for a tree just before Vinny had been kidnapped.

Tomorrow, when she had her head screwed on
right, she was going to go out and buy the best damn
Christmas tree she could find.

If there were any decent ones left on the day before
Christmas.

The movie came back on. She watched for a moment, then began clearing away the large plate from
the coffee table. She'd brought her dinner over from
the kitchen table in hopes of finally finishing it. Or at
least eating half. The change in venue hadn't stimu-
lated her appetite. And watching the Christmas classic

hadn't helped. Especially now that George Bailey was calling to Clarence, saying he wanted to live again.

George would get his wife and family back, but she was going to go on alone.

Alone except for the wonderful boy who was sleeping in the next room.

She stepped into the minuscule hall to check on him. The door was partially open and she could see him. He was sound asleep.

Someone knocked on her door. Dakota stiffened. Fear instantly leaped into her veins, then she laughed herself out of it, releasing the breath she'd caught. She was going to have to get used to hearing someone at the door without being afraid that Del Greco had managed to track her down.

Del Greco wasn't going to be tracking down anyone anymore.

Approaching the door, she called, "Who is it?" When there was no answer, she opened the peephole. All she could see was a lush expanse of green. What was going on here?

"Who is it?" she asked louder.

"Santa Claus. Ho, ho, ho, have you been naughty or nice?"

Her heart constricted as she recognized the voice. Rusty.

Her fingers trembled a little as she opened the door. Dakota called herself an idiot. She'd sent him on his way, what was he doing here? And why was she behaving like some elementary schoolgirl confronted with the class hunk she had a huge crush on? She

hadn't behaved that way when she was in elementary
school, worldly wise years before her time. This was
an awful time for a flashback.

He looked like Santa Claus.

From the top of his red cap to his long, flowing
white beard, down to his shiny black boots. The only
thing she recognized were Rusty's eyes. And his
mouth. The same mouth that had quickly turned her
into molten lava in a small motel room on the out-
skirts of Las Vegas.

She stared at him. He was holding a tree up that
looked about seven feet tall against him. "What are
you doing here?"

"Bringing Christmas to you." Without waiting for
an invitation, he walked in, carrying the tree in with
him. "When I brought you home yesterday, I realized
that you weren't ready for the holidays."

She didn't bother saying that she had a tendency
to leave things to the last minute, or that she'd
planned on getting the tree and gifts. She was done
with excuses. "Things got away from me."

She watched as Rusty stood the tree up in exactly
the place she'd chosen.

He crossed back to her, opened the door she'd just
closed and leaned over to pick up something. Only
then did she realize that he'd brought a sack with him,
as well. A sack bulging with gifts.

He hefted it over his good shoulder, just the way
Santa Claus would have done. "Good thing I've got
a workshop and elves. Those malls are damn

crowded.'' Taking the sack over to the tree, he began
to unpack the gifts and place them beneath the tree.

''Santa Claus doesn't say 'damn.'''

He looked at her over his shoulder. It felt a hell of
a lot better than it had, but it was still fairly stiff.
Because he was trying to perpetuate the image of
Santa Claus, he'd temporarily abandoned the sling.

''That's because Santa doesn't usually spend an
hour trying to locate his sleigh in a parking lot.'' He
dug toward the bottom of the sack. ''You'd be surprised what Santa says when he's really frustrated.''

He'd gone shopping for her son after she'd all but
told him to take a flying leap. Guilt gnawed at her,
taking out large chunks. ''You didn't have to do
this,'' she told him.

He rose to his feet again. ''Haven't you heard?
Shopping's good for the economy.'' He picked up the
sack. ''I figure I just sent it up another few notches.''

She could feel them starting again. Tears. No one
had treated her like this before. Ever. Not even Vincent. ''You're a good man.''

He inclined his head. ''Santa Claus has to be.''

She felt like tugging off his beard, but she re-
frained. ''And how about Russell Andreini?''

He smiled to himself at the sound of his formal
name. ''Nobody calls me Russell.''

Rusty was a boy's name, and he had been all man.
''Maybe someone should start.''

His eyes held hers. He wanted to take her into his
arms, ache or no ache, but he didn't want to frighten

her off the way he had yesterday. "Are you volunteering?"

"Maybe." She ran her tongue over her lips nervously. Measuring her words. "And maybe I was a little too hasty."

"About?"

She took a breath, warning herself to not back down. She was through running from something. It was time she ran *toward* something.

"About turning you down so flat yesterday." She wasn't accustomed to explaining herself, but he had more than earned an explanation. "You have to understand, everything has always come the hard way for me." She looked at him pointedly. "Especially everything I've ever wanted."

He touched her face softly. "It doesn't always have to be that way."

"I know." She felt foolish now. "But I was suspicious."

He tried to understand what she meant. "Of an ulterior motive?"

Dakota shrugged her shoulders helplessly. "Something like that."

"My only ulterior motive is that I want to wake up every morning and find you next to me. If I've frightened you, I'm willing to do anything I have to to make it up to you."

How could he even think that there was anything to make up? And how could she have run from someone like him? "You already have. You gave me back my son." She looked at his shoulder. "You took a bullet doing it. And you saved my life. If anything, I owe you debts that I know I can never repay.''

That was where she was wrong, he thought, beginning to feel for the first time since he'd entered that it was going to turn out all right. ''We could work on the installment plan.''

''Yes,'' she agreed. ''We could do that.'' Dakota caught her bottom lip between her teeth. A grin was beginning to take hold. A grin and a feeling of complacency that overwhelmed her. ''When would you like your first payment?''

Instead of answering her, Rusty began digging through his sack again.

Her eyes narrowed. She'd expected him to toss the sack aside, not to rummage through its folds. ''What are you doing?''

''There's one more present in here.'' He felt around the very bottom. The box was small and easily lost. ''I wasn't sure whether or not to put it under the tree.'' Finding what he was looking for, he pulled it out and held the box out to her. ''Now I am.''

She felt her throat go dry. He'd gotten her a ring. After she'd turned him down. Dakota raised her eyes to his. ''Is that what I think it is?''

He placed the box in her hands. ''Only one way to find out.''

She wanted to savor the moment. ''It's not Christmas yet.''

''I'm Santa Claus, I can let you bend the rules a little.'' When she made no move to open the velvet box, he leaned over and did it himself.

Dakota felt her heart pounding as she looked down at the perfect marquis diamond that caught the light from the television set and winked back at her. "Oh, God, it's a ring."

"In a box like that, you were pretty safe in assuming it wasn't a pony." He peered at her face. "Is that a good 'Oh, God' or a bad 'Oh, God'?"

"Good. Very good." Still holding the box in her hand, she threw her arms around his neck. On the screen, Clarence had just gotten his wings. Dakota felt as if she'd just gotten hers, as well. "I don't know what I ever did to deserve you, Russell."

"Easy, you were just you." And having her in his life was more than he had ever expected. His arms tightened around her, bringing her even closer. "Now, about that first installment."

She laughed, looking up at him. "I guess you're really going to give me that happy ending you promised me when we started out."

He remembered. He had said it to seal their bargain just before they'd left for Vegas. It felt like an entire lifetime ago. "I always try to deliver."

Her eyes shone. "Then get started."

"Yes, ma'am."

"One more thing," she interjected just before he lowered his mouth to hers.

"What?"

"I love you," she whispered. When his eyes lit up, she was filled with warmth. "I just thought you'd like to know. I didn't think I ever could again, but I do. I love you," she repeated.

He framed her face with his hands. "That's good to know, although I already love you enough for both of us."

She could feel a smile all but consume her. It was going to be the best Christmas ever. For her and for Vinny.

When Rusty began to lower his beard, she stopped him, her eyes shining. "What's it like to kiss a man with a beard?"

"Can't tell you firsthand." He smiled into her eyes. "But why don't you find out?"

She was more than up to the challenge.

*　*　*　*　*

Award-winning author
BEVERLY BARTON
brings you a brand-new book from her bestselling series!

JACK'S CHRISTMAS MISSION
(Silhouette Intimate Moments #1113)

Jack Parker was a good ol' Southern boy with a slow grin and a body built for passion. But nothing could have prepared him for his feelings for spirited Peggy Jo Riley, the single mother he was duty bound to protect. Now Jack was on a mission to make her his own. And he *would*—just in time for Christmas!

Available in November
from your favorite retail outlets!

Only from

INTIMATE MOMENTS™

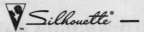

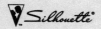

INTIMATE MOMENTS™

and NATIONAL BESTSELLING AUTHOR

RUTH LANGAN

present her brand-new miniseries

Lives—and hearts—are on the line when the Lassiters pledge to uphold the law at any cost.

Available November 2001
BY HONOR BOUND (IM #1111)

Eldest brother Micah Lassiter discovers the dangers of mixing business and pleasure when he falls for the beautiful woman he's been hired to protect.

Available January 2002
RETURN OF THE PRODIGAL SON (IM #1123)

Ex-C.I.A. agent Donovan Lassiter learns the true meaning of love when he comes to the rescue of a young widow and her two small children.

And coming in spring 2002
Mary-Brendan and Cameron Lassiter's stories

Available at your favorite retail outlet.

Where love comes alive™

Visit Silhouette at www.eHarlequin.com   SIMLL

COMING NEXT MONTH

#1111 BY HONOR BOUND—Ruth Langan
The Lassiter Law

Pru Street had no idea that her sexy new neighbor had been secretly hired by her father to protect her. But Micah Lassiter's hero status in the security business made him determined to keep the feisty graduate student safe from her stalker—and to welcome her into his passionate embrace!

#1112 BORN IN SECRET—Kylie Brant
Firstborn Sons

International spy Walker James was not happy when he learned that his partner in his latest assignment was former flame Jasmine LeBarr. Could the headstrong duo stop the threat of biological terrorism and rekindle the fire of their turbulent past?

#1113 JACK'S CHRISTMAS MISSION—Beverly Barton
The Protectors

Successful TV personality Peggy Jo Riley's life was in danger and she was forced to go under the guard of macho man Jack Parker. Now Peggy Jo's daughter was convinced that Jack would not only keep them both safe but that he would stay at their house for Christmas—and forever!

#1114 THE RENEGADE AND THE HEIRESS—Judith Duncan
Wide Open Spaces

Mallory O'Brien was running for her life when Finn Donovan found her in the snowy mountains. He vowed to keep her safe but soon discovered that protecting her from kidnappers was one thing, while protecting his heart was another altogether.

#1115 ONCE FORBIDDEN...—Carla Cassidy
The Delaney Heirs

Their love had once been forbidden—the rich girl and the boy from the wrong side of the tracks. Now Jerrod McKay was back in Johnna Delaney's life, asking for her help. Yet, how could she give him her assistance without exposing her most closely guarded secret

#1116 THAT KIND OF GIRL—Kim McKade

Colt Bonner had returned home for the first time in twelve years, and virginal Becca Danvers hoped to draw his attention. But Colt had always considered her to be just the girl next door. Could Becca convince him that he was the one man in her life she'd been waiting for?